SUMMERFIELD 3:

WINTER WARNING

BY

LAZETTE GIFFORD

Summerfield 3: Winter Warning
A Conspiracy of Authors Publication
www.aconspiracyofauthors.com
Copyright © 2021, AUTHOR
ISBN: 978-1-936507-99-3
Cover Art: Copyright © 20210, Lazette Gifford

First Print Edition, DATE

TABLE OF CONTENTS

CHAPTER 1

Despite our office at Woo Woo News -- excuse me, Wolton World News -- not being cold, I found myself huddling into my sweater as I sat at the computer. I tried very hard not to think about the new layer of snow falling outside the building, and I refused to look at the one window in the room. Winter didn't officially start for a few more days, but this year the first snow had begun around Halloween, and the weather hadn't improved since then.

The over-long winter was not entirely natural; many of the storms had coalesced around the Omaha area because of the inordinate amount of magic used in the city in the last few months.

Yes, magic.

We'd had an influx of fae in late summer. I would be tempted to say *infestation* of fae, even though I do rather like most of them. It is a good thing I get along with them so well since as of Halloween, I have assumed the role of Lord of the Fae.

This is kind of a problem for a human. I keep going over the events of last autumn and trying to figure out how this happened and why some of my fae friends still seem to think this is a good thing.

Today, though, I did my best to bury those thoughts and concentrate on my job as the top reporter for the top paranormal newspaper in the country. My current assignment was to find out information about an enormous white wolf that had been sighted several times in the area. We often get hoax reports to Woo Woo News, but I was fairly certain this was real, and the wolf was the shape-shifting totem of the fae's Wolf Clan. Tessa, my fellow reporter (and the Cat Clan totem) was out seeing if he could track the wolf down, though he sounded dubious about an actual meeting. I guessed it was the cat versus wolf aspect.

I shifted in my chair and nudged one of the sleeping pixies off my foot. It snarled softly and rolled over onto the pile of another four pixies. More were spread out around the chair. Tessa had managed a spell that hid them from humans, but I had to be careful not to trip over the guys. I feared people would think I had started drinking, but it turned out that my eldest sister, Rose, feared a complication from the car crash I'd had a few months ago. Technically, she was right since that was when I first saw the pixies.

I did not want any of my sisters worried and looking into my personal life. So I tried very hard not to trip over pixies and to break my fae friends of calling me *Lord Summerfield* in public.

Life had gotten strange, which was odd for someone like me to admit. My life had never been normal --

I couldn't say I was even surprised when Tessa rushed into the office we shared. I had been expecting trouble, but I had not expected Tessa to look so frantic.

"We have a serious problem, Summerfield!"

"The wolf?" I asked as he threw himself into the chair at his desk.

"Wolf?" he repeated, blinking as though the word meant nothing to him. "Oh. Him. Wolf Clan totem, just checking things out. No problem."

"Then what's wrong?"

"Winter Court," he said with a hiss of sound in his voice. Snow fell from his hair and coat. He shook his head, the worry not abating at so simple of words.

"This is a fae gathering?" I finally asked. The pixies were up and moving, agitated by what Tessa had said. "Why is this a problem now?"

Tessa took a deeper breath and then glanced at the doorway to the office as though he only now remembered that Julia or Pam might walk in at any moment. He pulled his chair closer to mine, a sweep of his hand sending the pixies back into a corner under my desk. They gathered there, a dozen or so, chattering and leaping up and down, some hitting the underside of the desk with their heads so that everything moved. If someone came in, they'd think we had a poltergeist. At least that would suit the office.

"Summer Solstice and Winter Solstice are the two major events in the fae world. Generally, those gatherings pass from clan-to-clan in a regular succession. However, when a new fae lord takes up a clan, that clan is the one to host the next court."

Oh yes, time to panic.

"I am not really --" I began.

Tessa caught hold of my arm and shook me. "Don't say that aloud. I know this is what you think, but don't admit to it. You must be *Lord Summerfield* or we're all in real trouble. We took our oaths to you, so now we either hold the Winter Court or admit you are not a Lord of the Fae and forfeit the power."

I wanted to deny this new madness. For Tessa to be this worried meant there was more to this problem than I could see. We ran into those sorts of things, where the fae simply didn't realize I didn't know the rules.

"If I lost my position as the fae lord, wouldn't things go back to the way they had been before?"

Tessa sighed and leaned back in the chair. "Nothing is ever that simple with the fae," he admitted. "If you fall from power, then everyone who swore an oath to you would be in danger of losing powers as well, depending on how the Queen of the Fae handled the situation. So far, she's ignored us, but that means she has also not confirmed you in your role."

We'd talked a little about this before, and everyone is content to let the confirmation slide as long as there were no repercussions.

"If you lost power," Tessa said and shook his head at the thought, "it wouldn't be just the fae here who could become weaker for it. Arinith might be affected as well and as a prince of the fae, that might could change things in the entire fae world."

"Damn." I felt the tide of panic start to well up around me. Pixies began leaping up and down hard enough to that I had to grab the laptop before it slid onto the floor. "Arinith shouldn't have --"

Tessa lifted his hand. He frowned slightly but at the same

time looked a little less worried. "Prince Arinith took an oath with you on his own, and he's been around long enough to know what sort of problems the new clan might face. We've done good things, Summerfield. We've no reason to regret our actions, so let's start working on making certain about the future. Desina, the Wolf Clan totem, mentioned the Winter Court in passing -- it was to remind me, which was a kindness I would not have expected. The others are more curious than anything, at least as far as I can get a reading on the situation. But I have the feeling...."

His eyes went a little odd, the pupil widening as he stared at something other than me or the reality around us. I'd gotten used to Tessa's visions, and at least this one was short. He focused on me once more.

"I suspect Gryn and Roan are spreading the word that you will *not* hold the Court because you don't dare."

Those two were not among my favorite fae. Gryn had been the Cat Clan's Warlord who had proved treacherous to his own Clan. Roan, the totem of the Centaur Clan, was his new best friend, and he'd taken refuge with that clan. Roan was a coward who would do anything underhanded rather than face an enemy. They probably worked well together.

"How the hell can I hold a Winter Court?" I finally asked. "Where could we even hold an event like that for fae?"

"Yes, that is the second part of the problem." He brushed the last of the melting snow from his hair. "The Winter Court must be held in your own lands. We have to hold it *here* and the court will last for five days."

I started to speak. Stopped. The wind blew hard enough around the building that I could hear the howl. I suspected

12/Lazette Gifford

that came from Tessa's mood.

"So, how many fae are we talking about?" I asked. I might have even sounded sane.

"As many as five hundred or more -- and I would guess *more* in this case. We're talking all the clan leaders, High Elves, and -- of course -- Queen Amata. The gathering lasts for five days, though not all day. It's an evening event until midnight of each day -- one day before and three days after the solstice. That would be the 20th through the 24th. We dare not make a mistake in this, Summerfield."

"You expect me *not* to make mistakes? I don't know nearly enough --"

"You can learn. We have to figure out how to do this. It's almost quitting time. We can meet with the others for pizza. They don't know yet."

"Tessa --"

"We are not giving up without a fight." His panic had already been replaced by the determination and stubbornness I was far more used to seeing.

Tessa scooted his chair back to his desk and began to scribble notes. I went back to looking at my files about the wolf. I knew the truth now, but it was not something I could use in the story. I had to be creative but still stick to the facts as we knew them. When, where, why: the first two were easy, the last I could suggest as a sign of nature, and not necessarily a problem.

When I looked back up, I found Tessa staring at me. He gave a decisive nod. "We will figure this out, or we will all go down together," Tessa declared.

I thought about all the trouble we would have with

around five hundred fae partying in Omaha.

Oh yes, time to panic.

CHAPTER 2

We finished our workday, and I reluctantly gathered my jacket, gloves, and hat to head back outside. The weather didn't worry me so much, even bad as it was, but I hated the idea of leaving the calm sanctuary of the office.

Yeah, writing for Woo Woo News was becoming the mundane part of my life.

Pam gave us a wave as she headed out the door, rushing toward her apartment in The Fortress -- a downtown building I had bought and we all lived, my fae followers and human friends and which was only a few blocks away. The humans did not realize they shared the building with magical beings from another realm, though.

Pam was used to Tessa and I heading off to other places after work, and she hated to have us drop her at home first. Pam had begun testing her new independence, and I respected it -- but I also had Tessa and the others make certain she always made it home safe.

Our boss, Julia, was just coming down from her upstairs apartment, and I could see flour on her shirt. The smell of fresh baked cookies drifted down the stairwell after her. The outer office where she and Pam worked had been quiet on such a blustery day, and Julia must have decided to get a head start on her holiday baking.

"Do you think six dozen sugar cookies will be enough for the Solstice Eve gathering? I baked four dozen last year, and they were gone before midnight."

"Julia, the truth is that no matter how many cookies you bake, we'll eat them all. Do you really want us waddling around her for the rest of the winter?"

She laughed, but I had the feeling it would be six dozen anyway. I had glanced at Tessa, though. He gave a nod. We had another complication with the office party.

"Looks like the weather is turning bad again out there," Julia said as the three of us moved to the outer door. It radiated cold and shook in the wind. "You two be careful."

"We will," I said and forced myself to shove open the door and head out into the cold. Tessa followed me and then moved to my side as we went around to the parking lot. Julia locked the door behind us and shut down the lower floor lights.

"We do not need more complications," Tessa mumbled.

"This isn't the only one we have," I replied as I managed to avoid tripping over pixies. They didn't much care for the weather, either. "I also have my family's yearly holiday gathering. At least Glynis has gone home for the holidays, so I don't have to try and explain this new craziness to her."

"I would think you were psychic for buying her that trip home for the holidays," Tessa said as we reached the Hummer and I keyed the doors opened. "This is going to be troublesome, Summerfield. And dangerous."

"I had guessed as much."

Tessa got in. I opened the door and waited for the pixies

to climb up and scurry to the far back, where they could look out like a herd of tiny dogs. They'd at least learned not to get underfoot while I was trying to drive. I thought Tessa was going to have a heart attack before we broke them of that habit, though. Tessa was barely used to me talking while I drive. Reaching down and grabbing pixies from the gas pedal and the brake was too much for him.

I climbed in and sat there, staring out the window and trying to fit this new madness into the rest of my odd life.

"You know, we'd get to the pizza place a lot faster if you would actually start the car and drive," Tessa suggested.

I checked to make certain there were no pixies under my feet and finally started the car and got us moving. The car slipped a little on a bit of ice, but the roads had been cleared, I was glad to see.

"Tessa, I don't know enough. I'm barely learning court etiquette to deal appropriately with the rest of you. Knowing the fae as well as I do -- which is far too well for a human -- I can guess that the Winter Court would mean protocol beyond anything I know."

"You're always polite enough," he replied with a wave of his hand. I pulled out onto the snowy street. There was not much traffic. "We can teach you what you need to know to deal with the Queen of Fae. She's a step up from Arinith's level."

"She can't be happy about my position, and especially not with Arinith taking an oath with me."

"She hasn't said anything yet, you know."

"She hasn't had to actually face me, either."

He didn't argue. I headed for our usual pizza place.

Driving wasn't so bad, especially with Tessa who made certain we moved when we should and stopped without sliding. I just had to make sure no one else was having those problems. The trip gave me some time to think about the situation, and I can't say I felt any better by the time we pulled into the parking lot.

"What do I need to know?" I finally asked.

"The other fae will watch for you to make mistakes and you don't dare. I'll help you learn the protocol. We can use magic to teach you the rules if we need to, but it's better if you learn them naturally. That's not going to be any trouble. The real problem is going to be finding a place for this gathering."

Hell.

The waitress and cashier both gave friendly nods as we entered. This was a spot we often stopped at after work to meet with the others. The place was packed as usual, though many of the people had probably walked over from the nearby apartments.

Kala, Brandis, York and Vane had a table in the corner. No matter how hard they tried to fit in, people seemed to sense that they just didn't belong here. It would take more than jeans and a lack of swords to make that transition.

I supposed I fit in better with my companions than I did with the locals. I had spent most of my life here in Omaha trying not to draw attention and looking around now, I realized I had failed miserably in that respect.

However, I gave a sigh of relief as Tessa and I had neared the table. I'd finally broken the others of their instinctive move to stand and bow whenever I came into the room. I had told them if they didn't stop, we would no longer be able to go out for pizza. Kala, Brandis, and York might not have thought much of the threat, but Vane took me seriously. Vane is the Dragon Clan Totem, newly reborn, lacking some of his previous memories, and closer to a human teen than his dragon form. Vane *really liked* pizza, and this was his favorite place. They did not deliver, and he wasn't stable enough to go out on his own.

The others looked happy, which meant they hadn't heard about the latest problem. Vane looked content, in fact, and I noted the debris of a pizza already consumed. Good. I didn't want Vane anxious before we even got to the problem.

Vane was not one of my people, but he lived with us and shared our problems. The remnants of the Dragon Clan, residing in my reality after a disastrous encounter with the Centaur Clan, had decided this was not the time to take their newly re-hatched shapeshifting dragon totem back to their own lands. Since I had been one of the people holding the square (a magic shield) when Vane had hatched, he was drawn to me. At least he grew fast, though he appeared to be slowing down in what seemed to be the late teens.

Kala glanced from Tessa to me and frowned. As the Cat Clan Warlord, she was proficient at picking up the subtle nuances of trouble. Brandis -- the Dragon Clan Warlord -- shifted uneasily as Tessa, and I took our chairs.

Tessa had settled between Vane and me on the right, with Kala on my left. He leaned forward and gave a grim nod. "You have probably realized there is a new situation. It's called the Winter Court."

"Oh hell," Kala whispered.

The lights in the place went out, then almost immediately sputtered back to life winning a scattering of laughter from the other patrons.

"Sorry, Sorry," Brandis said, and the others mumbled the same word. Even Vane, who had trouble with missing pieces of his memory as he grew back to what he had once been, seemed to understand the extent of the problem. York, always quiet, simply shook his head. The lights flickered again.

This was not the kind of reaction you wanted to see in people who faced trolls with glee.

The waitress brought another pizza, wisely putting it by Vane and more sodas. The others were starting to calm, though I did still see worry as they glanced my way.

"There are many problems related to this," Tessa finally said when we were alone again. "First is that Summerfield needs to know far more court protocol than we've taught him."

"That's the least of the problems we have," York replied. The Dragon Clan Bard usually kept quiet, but I could tell this one bothered him. "We don't have much time to get ready, and we don't even have a place to hold the event. Then there will be the problem of keeping Summerfield safe from all our wonderful fae companions."

"The Winter Court may be neutral ground, but nothing outside of it is, and that's proven to be dangerous at the best of times," Brandis added. he looked at me. "In case you haven't realized, this is not the best of times."

I nearly snorted the soda I was drinking as I laughed. That put the others in a better mood, too.

"You are so reassuring, Brandis," I finally replied. "I would like some pizza."

My companions reached, everyone ready to hand over all

the pizza and maybe grab some from other tables as well. Even Vane had moved as though he thought he needed to please me, even though he had never taken an oath with me. I sighed with frustration, and they all drew their hands back in haste. I pushed back my chair, preparing to stand to get my own pizza. The others started to move as well, ready to stand when I did.

"This is not a comedy routine, people. Calm down," I said and nodded thanks to Tessa who finally retrieved a piece of pizza and put it on my plate. He got a piece for himself. "Thank you. Let's figure this problem out."

"My first question is where are we going to hold this?" York asked. "We need some place big, fancy -- and not given to having humans wandering in and out."

"I'm sure all the hotels and convention centers anywhere in town are booked through the holidays." I took a bite of pizza and chewed slowly, aware of how the other watched him, waiting for Lord Summerfield to find an answer. "Let's assume we find a place. What other things do we need to worry about?"

Brandis started to protest, but Tessa lifted a hand, and Brandis fell silent. Even though the two shared a secondary clan allegiance, it was still odd for the Dragon Clan Warlord to take any sort of order from the Cat Clan totem. I saw flickers of surprise from the others.

"Summerfield is right," Tessa finally said. "We have to assume we'll find some place and work as though that will happen. Otherwise, when we do find a location, which might still take days, we won't have enough time to make the rest of the preparations. We don't have any time to waste. We need to get Summerfield, and ourselves, ready."

"The Summer and Winter Courts are neutral territories," Kala said with a bit of a snarl. "That means our enemies are bound to be there. Roan, since he's the Centaur Clan Totem, will make an appearance. Gryn might be there was well. We can't let them be a problem for us. In other cases, some of us would simply not go and avoid a confrontation, but we don't have that option. We need everyone there to make a strong show of followers, besides all the fae we'll need to keep things running smoothly."

"I would like to say you will be safe at the event itself, Summerfield," Tessa added. He picked up his pizza and put it back down. "I won't guarantee such safety this time. Besides, traveling to and from the Winter Court is not under any special protection."

"We have one more problem," I added and drew wary looks towards me. "Tessa and I have Julia's Summer Solstice party, and I have a family Christmas Eve gathering. Those all fall during the fae gathering. I could tell everyone that I am taking the holidays somewhere else, but that would make people unhappy, especially in my family. How would that affect my power structure?"

"Good question," York replied. He had begun playing with his pizza. "Your power rests not only with us but also with your relationship to your own world. We'll have to figure out a way around that one."

"That is what I suspected."

We drank in silence for a few moments while the others thought about the problems. Even Vane looked thoughtful while he ate another quarter of the pizza. The Dragon Clan stayed here for his sake, but the Cat Clan had lost their key to go home when Gryn turned on them. That was long before I came on the scene. However, if we held this event, other members of the Cat Clan who had never left the fae lands would be there. I suspected my Cat Clan friends would be able to go back home with them.

I said nothing. I'd want to talk to Tessa first.

"Oh," Kala suddenly moaned. "Court Dress! I can't remember the last time I wore a ball gown!"

I couldn't imagine it.

The others looked equally glum.

"Summerfield will have to take the first and last dance with Queen Amata," Tessa said. I put down my pizza again.

"I hope you know how to waltz," York added. He pushed his pizza across to Vane.

"In fact, I can waltz so I could dance with grandmother on her birthday. I was determined to do better than the others once I came to live in this area. I will need to brush up a bit. That's not a problem. The rest, though -- we have five days, my friends. We need to find our answers fast. I also need a lot more information if you don't expect me to make mistakes. What more do we need?"

"We need more pizza," Vane added.

The rest of the pizza had disappeared. I laughed and ordered another. Although we stayed late, we didn't come up with any answers, but at least the others had stopped panicking. Good. They left that part to me.

CHAPTER 3

We didn't return to The Fortress until just before ten that night. I pulled up to park out front since we had construction going on in the garage. Even though we hadn't come up with any good ideas on what to do, I began to relax for the first time all day.

The others had gotten to the pizza place in their own unique ways, but they rode home with Tess and me. Even Vane had taken to riding with us rather than flying. I thought he might like the company. Besides, the Hummer was warm, and I suspected Vane was not a cold-weather dragon. I'd have to ask one of the others since I knew so little about dragons.

I stepped out of the car and looked up at the building. This was home. People I trusted lived in the building, including those who had sworn an oath to me. There were also some others of the Dragon Clan who had not taken that oath, including Vane. They'd finally agreed that staying in the woods for the winter was not such a good idea since there was far too much of a chance they would be spotted. Brandis said they were all grateful for somewhere safe and warm to stay.

I had brought others in as well including Pam and her two daughters and Pablo, his wife, and kids. Others had moved out, complaining about the level clientele, but the place was better for having them gone. I liked it here and so did those who lived among the fae, though they didn't know about the magical aspects of their odd neighbors.

We headed up the walk to the building entrance when a car made a fast brake to a stop, far too close to us and the Hummer. My companions started to react, but I lifted a hand and stayed anything that might have been hard to explain.

I had recognized the car and wasn't surprised when Kenwood stuck his head out the window, brought up a camera, and started flashing pictures.

"Would you like us to pose?" I asked.

My companions laughed. Kenwood, who must have been watching us, wasn't amused. He also must have been nearby, waiting until we showed up. I was starting to get stalker vibes from the man, and that was not going to improve our relationship.

"You won't be such a smart ass when I get done," Kenwood replied with a snarl. He clicked a few more pictures, leaning farther out the window.

I saw Tessa's hand give a slight movement.

The camera dropped and broke.

"A shame about that," Tessa said as we turned and headed for the door.

Well.

I thought about telling Tessa that he shouldn't have bothered with Kenwood, but you know -- Kenwood was starting to *bother* me. I didn't need trouble from the human world along with the rest of this mess. Maybe if Kenwood lost enough cameras, he'd stop his childish crusade to annoy me.

I could hope, right?

Pablo watched from the doorway where he worked as a

security guard for the building during the day when we were apt to get odd visitors. He opened the door with a flourish that made me laugh as we hurried in out of the cold.

Oh yes, much better to be inside. Home. Safe.

Kenwood cursed rather loudly as the door snapped closed behind us.

"I'll keep an eye on him," Brandis said and stayed by the door with Pablo.

I knew better than to argue. Instead, I handed the box of leftover pizza (we managed to keep it out of Vane's hands) over to Pablo. He sniffed appreciatively. "I saw everyone's cars out there, so lock up when Brandis is done and get to your apartment. There shouldn't be anyone by this late in this weather, and if they are, they can buzz and wait."

"*Gracias*," he said. I think that was mostly for the pizza.

We headed past the elevator and to the stairs. Six steps lead down to the garage and the door there, but here the stairs headed upward. Another elevator, used mostly for furniture and such, sat at the far end of the garage. Fae rarely used elevators, though. Magic and technology sometimes don't work well, but I don't mind taking the stairs, especially after that much pizza.

Brandis reached us at the second-floor landing. He shook his head with distrust. "He's going to be a problem, Summerfield."

"Pest," I corrected. "Kenwood will be a pest. A problem is finding somewhere to hold the Winter Court. He's hardly even a distraction amid all the rest of this insanity."

"He's trying to make trouble for you," Tessa replied.

"Yes, he is. But what can he do? He has a bad reputation

as a reporter, especially after the last article got the newspaper in trouble. We need to make certain he doesn't harass anyone here, though."

We headed for my penthouse apartment. Though I live alone, the others wander in and out at will. The lower floor apartments were rented out to people I didn't often see, though two went to people I trusted -- Pam Jacobs and her children and the other to Rosa, Pablo, and their children. Another apartment was held by two of the Centaur Clan who had taken oath to me and had not gone back to their own clan, though they were not as ready to leap into the insanity with the rest of us.

I went to the dining room table -- a round table so we didn't have that 'head of the table' problem -- and sat down. York and Tessa went to the kitchen to make tea.

They are not servants. They'd made that plain enough early in our unique relationship. However, they were quite as capable of making tea as I was and, on a day when my head was almost spinning with worry, I appreciated it.

I had decorated for the holidays, with a nice tree in one corner and lights strung in other places. Wreaths hung over the windows, too. I enjoyed the festive feel of the place. Being here helped to calm me again.

When we had all gathered at the table again, I thought the others might have started coming up with ideas. I hoped so. We hadn't much time to pull this off.

"We can start working on the minor problems like dress and invitations," Tessa suggested, both his hands around his cup. "We need to get those things moving. Once we find a location, we can already have the rest of the stuff ready to go."

"So, I have to locate the place," I said and didn't' feel any better for it. I was going over every single location I could think of, but there was nothing large enough that wouldn't already be booked, though I would start calling around tomorrow to make certain.

"We do have one easy matter to settle, at least," Tessa said. "York should be the official bard for the event."

York began to frantically shake his head, unable to speak. I'd never seen him so flustered before, and we'd been in some dark situations together.

"I can't possibly --"

"You are more than good enough," Tessa insisted. "Far better than the last few I saw at courts. At the last Summer Court, I went to, the Wolf Clan Bard got drunk before the others even arrived. His totem ended up dragging him out of the building. Quite entertaining, but not the sort of thing we're looking for, I think."

"No wine for you," I said with a laugh.

York nodded emphatically, but I could see less panic on his face. I wasn't sure who else we would have gotten anyway.

"The Queen of the Fae brings her own court musicians," Brandis added for my benefit. "York will only play a few pieces, and he'll be a boon for us. People haven't heard him. They've no idea how good he is."

York blushed, but he appeared to be thinking through his part in this insanity. Getting the little things settled seemed like a good idea. I almost felt as though we were making progress.

"We can also handle the food and drink without a problem," Tessa added. He seemed to be thinking more clearly than the rest of us. "We can add a few exotic dishes, too. Most fae are not used to the variety of human foods that are available now. We can have a dizzying array of choices from various cultures. We will probably make a hit with those alone."

"And pizza!" Vane added.

The others laughed, but Tessa nodded. "Yes, I think pizza might be a good choice."

"We still need to come up with some place." Kala glanced out the balcony window as though she could find a location with a look. "This best not be somewhere that will not draw too much local attention, either."

"True," I agreed. "I don't want to have to deal with explaining any of this to my sisters. And that brings me back to the family gathering. I need to come up with presents for my sisters, too. I have shopping to do --"

"Bad timing," Brandis said with a shake of his head.

"I know, but I need to take care of these things. If any amount of my fae power rests on how people perceive me, then I don't think we want my sisters mad -- which means I must go to the family holiday gathering."

"This wouldn't be such a problem if it wasn't for the dates of the events."

"Speaking of dates," Tessa said and looked at Kala, "you are the best choice for Lord Summerfield's companion during the Solstice gathering if you both agree."

Kala had started to lift both hands as though to push the idea way, but she stopped in mid-move. "I would be the best to keep him informed and out of any obvious traps."

I nodded in agreement, glad that I would have someone close by who could help me through what was bound to be a series of metaphysical landmines.

"It's late," I added. "Let's get some rest and see what we have tomorrow morning. "Let's watch a show and head for bed."

We'd been watching holiday specials. My fae companions understood the religious implications of the upcoming holiday, but they were interested in the festive, cultural aspects. We watched *It's a Wonderful Life* and Kala especially liked how true to life the movie seemed to be.

I had to wonder about fae culture at this point.

Eventually, the others wandered away to their own apartments, a four of which designated for Cat Clan and Dragon Clan. I didn't ask how they sorted out who slept where, but I had noticed it didn't seem to be anything set. The few Centaur Clan who still held their oath to me had an apartment of their own, too.

Tessa had the apartment across from mine, which was often shared with Vane who might be in dragon form. They needed the room and had magically removed some of the inner walls.

Tessa stayed until the others were gone. He walked out on the balcony that overlooked the Old Market area of Omaha. They'd worked up a wonderful perpetual shield there that kept the area warm and at the same time hid someone standing there from view. They had also created a lovely 'no drone zone' around the building so Kenwood had stopped sending them up to try and spy on us. Tessa said they did the last with a pull of a breeze off the Missouri River, which was only about a block away. It looked quite natural.

I had to take the shield down on occasion and make an

appearance on the balcony so that the people watching -- and yes, they did watch -- saw me doing normal things. Not tonight, though. The snow had not eased, and I shivered watching Tessa, even though I knew he wasn't cold.

"There is a car parked down there across the street," Tessa said when he came back in. "A couple men inside which makes me think this is not Kenwood. He doesn't have friends."

"True," I said, rinsing out my favorite teacup to have it ready in the morning. "We can pull this off, right?"

"We have done the impossible a number of times already," Tessa reminded me as he closed the balcony and pulled the shades. "I don't see any reason to doubt that we won't pull this one off. This is going to be dangerous, Summerfield. The Winter Court itself is neutral ground, but there have been breaks in that truce in the past. We can't count on it, and we especially can't count on being safe while outside the area. If you didn't need to be seen elsewhere, we'd hold up wherever the festivities are held. Honestly, though, I don't think that would be any safer under these circumstances."

"I assume no one is happy about having a human as a fae lord. I'm not even sure it makes sense."

Tessa leaned against the counter. He looked contemplative this time. "I don't know that being human is the root of the problem. We've been five clans for eons: Cat, Dragon, Centaur, Wolf, and Eagle. The Summerfield Clan is different for a series of reasons because you have pulled us together from three different clans. We have no actual totem for Summerfield -- but you have me, and you might as well have Vane. You have an extraordinary amount of power in the people who follow you, from Totems to War Lords. Fae are reactionary."

"What do I need to do?" I asked.

Tessa frowned. Like the rest of my fae, he still had trouble dealing with our relationship. I was Lord Summerfield, but unlike other fae Lords, I needed considerable more information. I could see him fighting that moment when he fought the urge to say *whatever you think best.* I didn't know enough to make a reasonable decision.

"You need to minimize the number of places you go both before and during the Winter Court. People are mostly ignoring us, and I imagine a lot of them are curious to see what we do. Once the announcement is made, they'll start getting far more interested. You will need guards with you everywhere you go."

"Guards?" Things were already getting out of hand with this business. Fae guards going with me everywhere had been a problem in the past.

"You will have two honor guards at the festivities, too," he said and ignored that I had been about to protest. "That's normal. They're honorary but necessary, at least as a show of power. Don't worry. We're going to make this work. And you know, I think it's going to be damned fun once we get things figured out. We can handle this, Summerfield."

"Once we find a place to hold the event."

"Yes. That's the big problem, but I don't get a feel for that being our real problem." He gave a sudden nod. Brandis and I will be your Honor Guard."

"The Cat Clan Warlord is going to be my date, the Dragon Clan Warlord and the Cat Clan Totem are going to be my Honor Guards? You don't think this might be a bit over the top."

"Summerfield, you cannot possibly put on too much of a show for this one. The fae love a show, and you are going to be on stage. We'll put on a display they won't soon forget. Go get some sleep. You're going to need it."

CHAPTER 4

I awoke early the next morning with the distinct feeling that time was running out. We had four days until the Winter Solstice -- which mean we only had three days to prepare. I shouldn't be sleeping at all.

After a quick shower, I threw on some warm clothing and went out to the kitchen to make tea and bagels. The others would be here soon. I hoped they had come up with something helpful.

When I looked out the balcony windows, I could see another reason to believe nothing was going well. Had anyone predicted a massive amount of snow for the day or was this another reflection of how the fae were dealing with the current crisis in my life?

I sat down with a lovely cup of peach oolong tea and tried to force myself to be calm. Tessa arrived, got himself some tea, and sat down at the table with me.

He looked at the window and shook his head. "We need to get this in hand."

Which told me what I had already suspected; the fae were upset, and it was affecting the weather again. We didn't need a bad storm in the last week before the holiday. There were too many people who would be out and about and that would include me.

"Any ideas?" I dared to ask.

"We'll work it out," he replied, which was not a very reassuring answer. "We are a resourceful group, you know."

He was saved from saying any other platitudes and possibly patting me on the head, by the arrival of York and Kala. They carried in bolts of cloth and trim, which at least got my attention.

"We worked on the Summerfield colors last night, as well as some patterns for court clothing and banners," Kala explained. They laid out bolts of dark green and shimmering blue that looked like the sky. Gold trim landed beside it.

While Kala spoke, York weaved a little magic to show us the finished product. I had thought the colors looked gaudy, but the result was elegant instead.

"This is wonderful!" I told them.

"Yes, surprised us, too," York said with a laugh. "But we will not be going to the Winter Court looking like beggars."

"We just need to figure out where --" I started.

Tessa sat up straighter. "There's no place in the city. We need to search --" He stopped. The rest of us stopped moving and waited, but this did not have the look of one of his visions. "We have been limiting ourselves by thinking in human terms."

"You can create a place out of magic?" I asked.

"Oh yes, but that much magic in this area would not be a good idea. We can't take it to another realm, either." He smiled suddenly. Tessa always looked dangerous when he smiled. "Summerfield, define your lands for me."

"I never thought about it," I said with a frown.

"Neither did we," Tessa said. The others were starting to

look hopeful, but I wondered what he meant. "You are the only human lord of the fae, Summerfield."

"If he is going to make that claim, we had better do something official," York added. "Otherwise, one of the other fae might try to claim some of this world and push us out."

"True."

I had the odd feeling this might not be a good idea, but I knew we didn't have much choice since I suspected we had run out of alternatives. However, I remembered the last time I went along with one of Tessa's ideas -- and that was how I got to be Lord Summerfield.

We were already in this mess, and I needed to keep my people safe. I buried all those other worries and gave a quick nod of agreement. "What do I do?"

"There is an oath that new Lords take when they become the leader of a clan," York replied. It was probably his work, as a bard, to know these sorts of things. "Cross your arms over your chest and repeat these words: I, Sunflower Breeze Summerfield, do claim and accept my right as lord of all the human world."

"All?" I said with a slight squeak in my voice.

"We don't want to leave any backdoor open," Tessa explained.

The other two nodded. I thought they were insane, and maybe that was what happened to fae who were trapped in my world for too long. Maybe this was something I should seriously consider before I threw myself any deeper into this madness.

Hell.

"I, Sunflower Breeze Summerfield, do claim and accept

my right as Lord of all the human world."

Before I could take another breath, I felt something like a wind out of nowhere that swept through the room, displacing a few papers before it came rushing straight at -- and into -- me. I almost panicked, but in the next moment, the wind disappeared, and I felt only a little giddy.

"What the hell?" I asked. The others looked as confused and worried as I felt. The pixies began bouncing up and down, too. They looked excited, which I assumed could not be good.

Brandis rushed into my apartment -- probably not wise with other fae there. His hair dripped water down the front of his unbuttoned shirt. He looked as though he expected something to be lurking in the shadows.

"Summerfield just claimed the world as his lands," Tessa said. He frowned but then shrugged as well. "We figured that opened up our possibilities for a place to hold the Winter Court. I did not expect this to be more than a formality, but a lot of power just came with that oath."

I was about to ask if this was going to create more trouble -- stupid question, really -- when the trouble appeared.

I've mentioned the wards on The Fortress. They are strong enough that a stray mosquito couldn't get inside, which I rather appreciate in the warmer weather. They kept out anyone but those invited, except in the vestibule where we kept Pablo at the door to keep any eye on things. Otherwise, the meter reader and anyone delivering mail couldn't get inside, and that would lead to questions.

No one came any farther without my permission.

Except someone just appeared in the room. One blink and the stranger stood there; tall, dressed in an ancient Middle

Eastern style, with his hair and beard braided.

My people started to move.

Stopped.

Yeah, anyone who could walk through those wards was not someone to mess around with, especially when it came to magic. He glanced around the room and gave a short nod. With a wave of his hand, his skirt and cloak disappeared, replaced by pants and shirt. Magic, but not the kind fae used. I could tell that much from the feel. He tried to look as though he fit in, but there was something odd about the man that went beyond his ability to walk through wards.

"So, *little one*, you think you can claim the world as your own now?" he demanded. His voice reverberated through the room. "We shall see."

He turned and walked away from the reality of my dining room. We all stared, and my heartbeat began to slow again. Tessa, I noted, looked appalled.

"What happened?" I finally asked. "Who was that?"

"I don't know," Tessa admitted. Brandis grabbed a chair and sat down. So did the others, and with me still standing. "Whoever -- whatever -- he was, he just passed through the wards as though they were nothing --"

"I noticed that part." I finally sat down as well.

"He is dangerous," Brandis said and still stared at the point where he had walked away.

"We don't need dangerous," I protested, for all the good that would to us."

"Nothing we can do about it now," Tessa said and shook his head. "If you renounce the lordship of this world, we'll have trouble with the fae. They'll have caught what we did by now, and we don't dare back down. So far, the other problem is ... talk and potential for trouble. We'll work on what we can to avoid that one, but we have other problems to face."

I gave a nod and turned my wandering (some might even say frantic) thoughts back to the first problem. We still hadn't come up with a place for the Winter Court. I also needed to learn more fae etiquette.

Oh, and at some point in the next few days, I had better finish my Christmas shopping.

CHAPTER 5

While the others moved in and out of the apartment, doing whatever fae things needed to be done, I sat down at the table and made a list of what I still needed to do. Top of the list was trying to find some unique gifts for my sisters. This was a yearly challenge for me, and though I probably fret too much over it, I do like it to matter. I've seen too many people rush into stores, buy the first things they find, and give no true thought about the gift-giving part.

I went to the desk and looked through things online but found nothing I liked.

"I need to go out and do some work today, Tessa," I said. He frowned, of course. "I'll do what I can online, but there is a matter I must see to in person today."

Tessa started to argue and changed his mind. "Brandis and I will go with you. We dare not be lax now since the fae world will have heard about what we did."

Kala had been standing by the window for a while, and she turned now, looking bothered. "We have people watching The Fortress," she said with a wave towards the street below "Humans and they have tech equipment."

"That sounds like trouble." I crossed to the balcony and looked out.

"There and there," she said, pointing to an old van and a newer sedan. "I don't know what they're doing."

I stared for a moment, as though I could see through the metal of the vehicles. "Leave them alone," I finally decided. "They're likely police or some other government group, and we don't want to give them a reason to want to come inside. We don't need this complication."

"Surveillance," Tessa said with a nod. "Their equipment won't get past the wards, but we need to be careful what we say outside the building. I have a feeling --"

Tessa crossed back to the table and pulled out his tarot cards, quickly laying them out in an arcane pattern that I had not seen before. Tessa touched a few of the cards and frowned.

"Yes, we're in trouble," he said with a quick nod.

"You needed to do a reading to find that out?" I said with a slight laugh. "We have the Winter Court, Julia's Solstice Gathering, The Summerfield family party, some ancient guy popping in and out of The Fortress, and now we seem to have the interest of some government group. What part of this did you think wasn't going to be trouble, Tessa?"

He laughed as he swept the cards up and put them back in his pocket. "I was actually hoping to find something that was less trouble. All I saw was potential disasters, but nothing seems set."

"That's good at least," I admitted. "I looked out the window but not at the cars again. "I'm trying to think of some place outside the city, though not too far because I don't think we want to be on the road --"

"We can always build a port," Tessa replied. "That's how

the others will get there from the fae lands anyway. We'll have to be careful about the magic and the weather, though."

"How far can we go with this port?"

"Anywhere on Earth. They take a lot of magic to build, but with a group our size, that won't be a problem. Once they're activated, they are easy to maintain, at least for a few days."

This gave us far more possibilities. We had some places that might not draw as much notice. "Does the Winter Court favor snow?"

"Yes," Tessa said with a sigh. He did not love snow.

"Good. We can start looking for some place in the Arctic Circle. Would you people have trouble creating an ice palace and keeping it hidden from satellite and plane view?"

Tessa looked more pleased than I expected, given that I was suggesting we went somewhere even colder and with more snow than we had here.

"This could work," Tessa said. "We can find an area and keep it clear of humans far easier than we could anywhere around here. Magic causing weather changes will be less noticeable there, too."

"It would be a perfect choice except for the cold," Kala added. "I suppose a nice, tropical island is out of the question?"

"They tend to be busy this time of year," Tessa reminded her.

"Damned humans always getting in the way," she said with a laugh.

"Oh, there's something more," I said. "We can move across the International Date Line. This will give us less time to prepare but will offset some of the events that I need to attend here."

"Yes," Tessa said with a quick nod. "We can do this."

Tessa and the rest of the fae began listing out the things they needed to do, which started with making the port. They'd put it in the garage behind the building project where it wasn't likely to be noticed, even when open.

I was running out of time for other matters, though. "I need to go out and handle something," I said as I stood. They all went still. "I'll make this as short a trip as possible, but I've already made arrangements --"

"Brandis and I will go with you," Tessa said. "The others are already starting the work here. The more we do, the more attention we draw -- so you need the guards now. You aren't going to argue, are you?"

"No," I said and went to get my coat, hat, and gloves. "Dress for the weather or people are going to think we're odd. And remember that we have those people in the van and car watching. I assume they're still there?"

Brandis looked out and nodded.

They dressed in coats and hats much like mine. The others watched us go with a little worry. I didn't like to think we would run into trouble, but I wasn't going to take any chances.

We went down the stairs, and Pablo met us at the door. He looked out at the weather and frowned. "*Policia* of some sort, Summerfield," he said with a nod toward the van. "What do they want? What are they doing here?"

"We're an odd group," I said with a smile. "Don't let them bother you. We're fine here."

He nodded but there was still distrust in the look he gave the van. Someone with his background was bound to be uneasy under the circumstances. I had learned that Pablo and his wife were both legal immigrants, but I would have fixed it anyway.

Pablo pushed the door open, and we stepped out. The cold wind hit hard, and I shivered ... and tried not to think about Arctic Circles and ice palaces. I'd apparently gone insane. No surprise there.

Brandis had paused slightly, and I saw his hand move toward the two parked cars. He caught up with us in the next two steps and gave a nod, though I wasn't certain what it meant. We didn't stop to chat until we were in the Hummer.

"Human, without a doubt," Brandis said as he settled in the back seat. "and no, they can't hear us clearly in the car any more than they can hear us in The Fortress."

"That's going to make them all the more suspicious," I warned.

"Can't be helped," Tessa replied. He took the seat next to me, and Brandis settled behind us. The pixies -- I was getting far too used to them -- had scrambled into the back. I had the feeling they liked going for car rides. Part of me wished the guys watching could see them. That would have been an interesting reaction.

"We'll rig up something so they get occasional safe stuff," Brandis added. "That won't be difficult. Right now, they probably think they have faulty equipment, though. I've seen that with humans before."

"I wish I knew what triggered this," I said as I started the car. "Though I guess I was right with what I told Pablo. We are an odd group. Try not to look dangerous."

"I'll refrain from changing into a cat," Tessa replied. "That's about the best I can do."

I gave a grunt of agreement and started the car out onto the street. Was it the Summer Fields Forever Foundation that had drawn attention? Most of the people in the building worked for the Foundation which was dedicated to preserving and creating wetlands and wildlife habitat. In fact, the fae loved the idea, and they were excellent at helping set up our few little buys so far. I saw it as a growing business and even my eldest sister, Rose never questioned it. What had started as a cover for all my odd friends was turning into something we were all happy to take part in.

I drove past the van. No one sat in the front, and I couldn't see into the back -- some sort of wall there.

"Maybe we should talk to Lenz," Brandis suggested.

"Let's not draw attention to him unless we have to," I replied.

I looked in the rearview mirror. The car was following us, which made me a lot more nervous than I liked. I almost suggested they have a little mishap, but I didn't think that would be wise.

We made it to the bank without any trouble. Mr. Harris, the manager who handled all my accounts, must have been watching carefully. He practically met us at the door, though he did give my two companions looks of distrust. It was a good thing he could not see the Pixies.

We went back to his office. I sat across from him, and after a little chat, he put a briefcase on the desk, turned it, and gave me the key. I opened, made a brief check of the money, and signed for it. Harris looked relieved when we walked away. I had the feeling Brandis and Tessa were far less so.

"You could have warned us," Tessa said as we headed out of the building and toward the Hummer. "What the hell are you doing?"

I smiled, noting the car across the street. They probably picked that one up, and I didn't even care.

"I do this stuff every year," I said. "Which means I've done it without the two of you."

"I've never seen so much money," Brandis admitted as he carefully sidestepped one of the pixies. They were trying to trip us until Tessa leaned down to brush something off his shoe and gave them a quick hiss. They lined up and were very careful after that.

"For this work, I don't want to leave a credit trail." I climbed into the car, started it up, and pulled out. The car was two behind us at the first light. "We are going to a private meeting with someone who will likely be nervous. Try not to do anything odd."

"You keep saying stuff like that as though you expect us to do something strange," Brandis replied.

Tessa laughed.

"This is the only business I need to do today," I said, which made them happier. "We'll deliver this to my guy from the utility company and head for home."

"Good," Tessa said and relaxed a little. "You'll have plenty of time to practice court etiquette with Kala."

"Or I could head to the airport and book a flight to the Bahamas after all."

"I like that idea," Brandis replied as he sat back. "It would be a really different place for the Winter Court. And yes, we would follow you there."

"I had that feeling. I'm not so worried about the Winter Court now that we at least have an idea of where to hold it."

"Now we're just down to doing what we can with magic," Tessa said. "And the truth is, this group has magic to spare. I would have liked more time --"

"No," Brandis said. "More time would just have meant more time to worry about everything. I'll be happy just to have it done."

Tessa nodded.

I glanced at the rearview mirror. Yes, trouble still followed us.

CHAPTER 6

I had to drive back across town, which meant dealing with the holiday traffic on Dodge, cutting through some side streets to get past the worst of it, and keeping an eye on the car behind us. They had to realize that we knew they were following by now, right? Did they hope to make us nervous? Were they trying to figure out why they couldn't hear inside the Hummer?

At the next stop sign, the wind hit with a sudden gust that even bounced the Hummer slightly.

"Looks like more of a storm coming in," I said, looking up at the sky. "Is this from you guys?"

"Some of it," Tessa admitted. "We've had a few bad shocks here in the last few days, but everything should calm down again soon."

"Now that we have things to do, it will help," Brandis added. "It's probably good that we're going to get back early, though. I get the feeling...."

I hated when fae just stopped talking like that in the middle of something that might be important. I sighed, but it was Tessa who looked at me and nodded.

"There is something more working on the weather," he said, and I saw Brandis lean forward and give a quick nod. "Something other than the fae."

"We don't need anything else," I mumbled and they both grunted agreements. "At least we will be done with all of this soon."

"Then we'll be fine until the next problem," Brandis replied, which was not exactly what I wanted to hear. "We al know there is going to be more trouble, right? Though the whole Winter Court problem isn't as bad as I feared it would be."

"You seem to be doing well here," I said and slowed down as a car spun out ahead of me. Tessa shook his head, used a little magic, and got them going the right way again. We made it to the light just as it changed. "I sometimes forget that the Dragon Clan hasn't been here nearly as long as the Cat Clan."

"And most members of the Cat Clan hid away until recently." Tessa shook his head and looked out at the world as cars sped by in front of us. "I can't say they weren't wise. Even I kept my distance in some ways, but I was drawn to the human world."

"By your visions?" I asked.

"Some," he admitted. I didn't realize what they meant until things started falling together last summer. We are doing well, Summerfield, but I don't like the odd visitor we had, and I can't get a fix on what he might even be."

"Maybe we can talk to Arinith at the Winter Court," Brandis suggested while I carefully pulled out, watching for anyone who might not be stopping as well as they expected. "This guy feels as though he might be related to that type of being, but more powerful."

"I don't need to hear that," I mumbled. "I don't need him

to be any more trouble than he already has been."

"He's an unknown," Tessa said and looked bothered. "We don't need another level of unknown in this mess."

I couldn't argue with Tessa's reasoning. Besides, even I was getting an odd feeling about all of this. I concentrated on driving.

"You know, I'm looking forward to the Winter Court," Tessa confessed. I gave him a look of such shock and horror that he started laughing. That didn't help.

"I apologize," he finally said and patted me on the arm. "I just haven't been to one in a long time."

"And this one is going to be interesting," Brandis added. "If we weren't all so involved in the panic side of the event, we'd probably be really interested in watching what's going on here."

"Which means we are all on show and that's adding more pressure," I said.

"True," Brandis agreed. "I hadn't considered how this must be affecting you. My apologies."

"I'll do fine," I replied. "Now that things are starting to fall into place, I'm already feeling better."

I could still see our tail was only a car behind us again. At least driving through town let us see some of the decorations, though most of them would look better at night. I loved the festive feeling in the air. I pointed out a snowman family in one yard: parents, three children, and even a cat and dog. The artist had done a wonderful job. I thought Tessa and Brandis appreciated it just as much as I did.

We stopped at another light. The cold wind blew harder again, and I saw snow start to fall from one breath to the next.

Oh yes, we needed to hurry back to The Fortress as soon as I took care of the second part of this business. I hoped the weather didn't turn worse. I did not want to be on the road with a horde of crazed holiday shoppers all trying to outrace the storm.

"That looks miserable," I said, with a wave towards a shopping center and the lineup of cars already trying to escape. "The temp is dropping, too. I wish I had a nice hot cup of tea."

And a cup of hot tea appeared.

Unfortunately, I had just eased down on the gas, and this wasn't exactly the right time for me to grab a cup popping up in the air in front of my face.

"What the hell!" I slapped the cup away. Tea went flying. I almost lost control of the car, but I caught tight hold of the wheel and eased my foot off the gas before I slammed into the little Subaru in front of us. "A bit of warning next time, guys!"

I saw Tessa glanced into the backseat and Brandis.

"That wasn't me," Brandis said.

"It wasn't me, either," Tessa added. It wouldn't be. He hated when I got distracted while driving. He lifted a hand and brushed up the tea and cup, and it held it in his hands.

I had started to slow the car down because I was trembling for some reason. I was used to magic. This shouldn't have unsettled me so much.

"The magic came from inside the car," Brandis said. He sounded worried. "The pixies haven't picked up that much magic, have they?"

Tessa turned to stare at the little guys in the back. He lifted a hand and looked hopeful, which I thought was crazy. I didn't want pixies around with that kind of magic.

"Not the pixies," he finally admitted.

Cars honked behind us because I had slowed down again. This was getting worrisome. I got us through another cross street before I turned my attention back to Tessa -- just a quick glance his way, but I could tell we had problems. He looked, very, very worried.

"If it wasn't either of you two, then who did the magic?" I asked.

"Oh," Brandis said, and now he sounded worried. "This could be real trouble."

"Tessa?" I said.

Tessa didn't say anything for a moment. He stared at the cup and finally placed it in the holder between us. I glanced at the cup, which looked suspiciously like my favorite.

"Tessa?" I said.

"This is a problem." I saw him shake his head, as though he couldn't quite figure out what to say. "This is another oddity at a time when we don't need any more problems. Summerfield, I want you to drive to where we are going. Concentrate on that work. And do not wish for anything aloud."

"I didn't do the magic!" I protested. We'd stopped at another light. I took several deep breaths to clear my head and maybe stop the trembling. "I don't have -- No, it can't be me. I don't have any power."

I drove on. Tessa said nothing and Brandis remained equally silent. A glance at the pixies showed them rather unsettled, staring back at me. We didn't have much farther to go, though. I found a spot to park within two blocks. We wouldn't have far to walk to the cafe.

"How do you feel?" Tessa finally dared to ask.

"Tired and shaky," I admitted as I leaned back. "What the hell happened?"

"I have a theory," Tessa said and lifted a hand towards me as though to feel something, though he never touched. "But his is only a theory because I have never heard of anything like this happening before."

"Something new and unusual going on around me? Who would have expected such a thing?"

He gave a little laugh. "You are right. This is what I think. You are already linked to magic through us, Summerfield. I think you may have made yet another connection to magic when you became the Fae Lord of this world."

"You mean --" Brandis began, and then stopped as though he didn't want to say what he thought. I stared at the steering wheel. Brandis finally leaned forward. "You think he has magic?"

"I think he can use magic," Tessa corrected. "Unfortunately, this looks like a very dangerous drain on his body."

"Like when I had the Key?" I asked.

"That's my theory," Tessa replied. He ran a hand through his hair. "I will learn more, but you need to consider a few things right away. First is that you were lucky that your 'wish' wasn't simply for hot tea, but rather a cup of hot tea. Otherwise, there would have been hot tea pouring on you. That could have been a real problem if we'd been moving."

There was something to consider. "I have to say the words aloud, though, right? I have wished for things in my head all day, but it hasn't affected anything."

"Good. Magic is usually keyed to words, and the words then trigger an action. Otherwise, the fae would be in a constant state of flux."

That was another good point. I relaxed a little, though the idea that I didn't dare say certain words aloud worried me. I wasn't used to thinking about the everyday things I said.

"You were also lucky that you were dealing with inanimate objects in this case," Tessa added. He sounded worried. "Those take less power to manipulate. If you had wished for something that included a live object, it could put a dangerous drain on you. You might get a dog to stop barking for an hour, but I suspect you wouldn't be able to do much else for the rest of the day. Wish for something related to a human, and you would use considerable power. You might not survive it."

Oh, now there were more good things to know. I sighed and glanced at Tessa at the next stop sign. "I don't need anything weirder in my life."

"I'll find out what is going on. We'll figure this out," he said. He sounded too nearly panicked to settle my nerves with those worlds. "Let me give you a little boost like I used to do when you were still holding the key."

I gave a distracted nod and drove on. Tessa picked up the cup, infused the damned tea with a little magic, and handed the cup to me. I sipped and felt better. Nothing bad had happened, right? Odd, but not bad so far. Tessa and the others would figure something out.

"Now what?" I asked.

"We go on with what you planned," Tessa said. He still

looked frazzled, and a glance at the mirror and Brandis didn't help. I was used to the Warlord of the Dragon Clan looking stoic, not shocked, and worried.

I concentrated on the mundane work at hand. Right: giving $100,000 away was normal stuff. Still, I could get this done and then get back to The Fortress. I took deep breaths again, accepted calm into my body and soul, and found a place to park. We were good. This wouldn't take long.

The car that had been following us took a quick turn into an alley. I wondered if we should wait for them, maybe buy them some coffee while I took care of business. Following me around all over town had to be pretty boring.

I got out of the car and my two guards leapt out to join me, as did the pixies. They managed to trip Tessa but retreated quickly before he got back up. "I'm going to make this as fast and easy as I can so we can get back home."

They both agreed with nervous looks around. I took the briefcase from Tessa and headed to the little cafe at the end of the block. The sidewalk had spots of ice, and I almost went down twice, but Tessa caught hold of my arm each time. Great. I probably looked drunk or drugged. The pixies were sliding along and having a snowball fight, but at least they were invisible. The bits of flying snow looked as though it was falling off of buildings and splashed up by passing cars. They were having fun. Maybe they'd get tired out.

My mind had been working on other things, though. "This is going to sound odd --" Tessa and Brandis both made amused sounds "-- but I get the feeling that I know the guy who walked into my apartment. Yet, at the same time, I know that's not possible. He is not one of you, and I certainly didn't know anyone else like that before I met your groups."

"Perhaps there is some link between the two of you," Brandis said. "That might be a way to trace who he is if we can figure out the link."

Tessa put a hand on my arm and stopped me while a group of people hurried past. I glanced back and thought someone might be close to the Hummer. I suppose they were trying to figure out how to hear what we were saying when we were inside. I supposed they had put a bug on the car. That must be frustrating.

"Summerfield, I want to put a shield around us to keep you from accidentally using magic that might affect others," he murmured. "We can't be certain this is only prompted by wishes. I don't think we dare take a chance."

"Good point," Brandis said.

"Will this be a problem for you, Brandis?" Tessa asked, which reminded me that they were only linked through me, though each had their own clans.

"No problem," he replied with a quick smile. "We'll be slowed down in reacting to any threat, but I don't think it will be a significant loss of time. I don't want anything unusual to happen out here in the world. Let's do it. I'll take care of the spell. You keep an eye on Summerfield and our other friends."

They were not giving me any choice in this, but I didn't mind.

A gaggle of teen girls swept past us, giggling, and making eyes at us. I thought of my sisters at that age ... and shuddered at the thought of them acting like this. It just was not possible. And that, of course, made me think about the upcoming holidays. Just far too many things going on.

"Keep an eye on whoever has been following us," Brandis said. "We have guessed that they are government, but there are others who might be far more dangerous."

I glanced back. People lingered near the Hummer. We might have to let them listen in on something innocuous to keep them from going crazy wondering why they couldn't hear anything at all.

We walked on to the cafe, the spell working in around us. I felt cold and unsettled, and I really didn't need this new level of weird. I also didn't used to have any trouble with the idea of walking down the street, even with a considerable amount of cash in hand. Today, though, everything felt out of place. Maybe that was just me, and I no longer fit into this world.

The cafe smelled of fresh bread and coffee. I inhaled the normality of it and realized that not everything in the world had gone bad. I even smiled as we neared the table where the man sat.

This was the first year with the pixies, not to mention my other friends. The pixies wanted treats, though. They would at least behave.

He looked up, nervous -- and I realized it was not me, but the company I kept today. I had never brought anyone with me before, and even under normal circumstances, Tessa and Brandis would have been daunting on the best of days.

"Tom," I said with a bright smile and held out my hand. We shook, but he still gave the other two worried glances. "This is Tessa and Brandis. They decided to tag along today. I don't think they trust me out alone with this briefcase."

Both Tessa and Brandis started to protest, though all three of us knew it was true. I laughed, and Tom looked far more at ease now.

We took the other chairs, ordered coffee and cookies. I saw that two men entered the cafe, but I couldn't be certain if they were the ones who had followed us or not. I decided not to worry about it, but I could tell Brandis had placed himself to keep an eye on them.

Once the coffee and cookies arrived, Tom pushed three papers over to me. Both Brandis and Tessa twitched, but I don't think he noticed. Most years I would have liked looking at the list of names and the short notes on the side to understand what good I was doing in the world. I felt tempted to rush, glance it over, nod, and give him the money.

Tom deserved better. He spent a considerable amount of his own time putting this together. I wouldn't belittle his work.

"Excellent as always," I said a few minutes later. I'd been able to eat three cookies and carefully provide the pixies with cookies as well while I read, which had helped. I would rather have had tea than coffee, but at least it was hot and full of caffeine. "Thank you for all the work."

Tom looked at me, his eyes narrowing slightly. I wondered if there was another problem.

"Why do you do this?" he asked.

"Because I can," I said with a slight shrug. "That probably sounds trite, but sometimes it is reason enough."

"It wouldn't be for most people."

"I am not like most people." I laughed when my two companions gave frantic nods of agreement. Tom smiled as well. "I have the money to help. That should be enough."

I suspected he really didn't understand. No matter. I didn't think I could explain this any better. Looking at my two companions, though, I had the feeling they understood better than Tom. I suspected that most of the fae tried to do things for the right reasons and not just for personal gain -- or at least my companions were that way.

We talked for a little while longer. When we were ready to go, Brandis stood first and glanced around the area. "I'll walk you to your car," he said with a nod to Tom. "And the two of you can head back to the Hummer."

He tried not to make it sound like an order, but Tom got a worried look on his face. "Are these two guards?"

"Overzealous friends," I replied, without actually saying that they were not guards. "They take things very seriously sometimes. Is your car nearby?"

"Out the door and to the right," Tom replied and gave Brandis a worried look.

"He's being careful," I said. "Things have seemed odd today."

There was one of my better understatements, I realized. I had become a Fae Lord of the World. I used magic. Odd was not quite the word that could encompass the kind of day I'd had so far.

The men I suspected of following us had left just moments before us, which made me even more suspicious. Brandis was right to take care because we really didn't know what was going on here.

I put a $100 bill on the table as a tip and saw Tom give me an odd look.

"Because it is the holidays," I said. "And is going to make someone happy."

He smiled and walked out beside me, with Brandis ahead

and Tessa behind. I did think they were more than a little over the top with this, but there was no reason to take chances.

We stepped out into the cold -- colder, in fact, than it had been barely half an hour before. The wind blasted down the street and snow fell in a white sheet that blocked the view half a block away. I started to glare, but then I thought it might be okay. I felt protected, with fewer people likely to see me. Besides, people on the streets were going to be heading for home. That sounded good as well.

We walked Tom to his car, and he got in with a nod and a nervous glance at the briefcase. Over the next few days, he would pay a few bills off at a time so that it didn't all fall into the system too quickly and draw attention. He had done this for a few years, but he still looked worried when he accepted the money.

"Thank you for taking care of this," I said when he rolled down the window. "This isn't the sort of thing I can do without drawing attention for all the wrong reasons."

Tom gave a last nod and pulled away without any trouble after Tessa put a touch of magic on the car, though he had to step outside our shield to do so. I thought someone at the end of the street watched Tom go, but no one seemed to be following him.

"Let's get in out of the weather," Tessa suggested. "And get back home. We need to get settled in where I can do some study."

I agreed, hurrying back to the car, the pixies scrambling in ahead of us. They really didn't like the cold much. The Hummer felt solid, and as soon as I kicked the heat on, I thought maybe a nap, right there in the car would not be such a bad idea.

I felt as Brandis dropped the other spell, too. All three of us gave a sigh of relief.

"You felt that?" Brandis asked.

"Yes," I said and finally started thinking about driving away.

"Odd," Tessa replied with a shake of his head.

"Odd is the word for today." I stared at the storm and then turned so I could see both Tessa and Brandis. The pixies were already sleeping in their back corner. "Look, maybe I'm imagining things, but does it seem to you that the weather is not right?"

Tessa and Brandis both lifted their hands. Tessa was the one who nodded first and acted a bit more nervous. That didn't help.

"There is the feel of something out there. Subtle," Tessa explained. "Something has a hand in this weather, but not so much that it is overpowering what would be normal. What do you feel?"

"A sense of something not quite right," I said. I finally got us out of the parking spot and into the street. I did not look forward to driving in this weather, though. We had a long way to go back to The Fortress.

Might be his new connection to the world," Brands suggested after a couple blocks.

"Yes, maybe," Tessa said and tried to sound optimistic. "I wish I understood more. I am sorry if I have gotten you into something that is more dangerous than we expected."

"Everything is dangerous," I reminded him. "We simply have to do what we can. I hope the others have started coming up with answers. We don't have a lot of time to get this settled."

At the next block, the weather dramatically changed, going from snow to rain in one heartbeat. I wasn't the only one who hit my breaks, skidding on snow, ice, and rain.

"What the hell?" I snarled --

And then I saw the reason.

The man who had walked through the wards at The Fortress stood across the street, staring at us. He remained dry and warm in the midst of the atmospheric turmoil he'd created. I worried that others would see him as well.

"Get us out of here," Brandis ordered and sounded both annoyed and worried. "Head to The Fortress. If it looks as though we can't get there, head for Fontanelle Forest."

"Do you think we'll be safer there?" I asked, watching as I drove far too close to the man. Oh yes, he watched, anger and distrust in his eyes.

"No, not safer," Tessa replied. "but we will have fewer witnesses to deal with if we have to do something . . . odd."

Another good point. However, a few yards away from the man and the warm wind turned cold again, leaving a sudden sheen of ice on the windshield. Tessa put his hand to the glass before I could even curse, and the ice melted away. I tried not to worry about the others on the road as well, but from the way Brandis watched behind us, I suspected they would be safe.

I didn't race back to The Fortress. I did consider abandoning the Hummer and having my friends get us there by magic. However, the Hummer would be found, and my sisters would be worried. Not the sort of thing I wanted to deal with when we had so many other problems.

We made it back. We'd lost the car tailing us somewhere, probably back in the freakish weather. I didn't worry about them. They would show back up before too long. The old van still sat there, and I had an inane urge to wave.

We went into the building, Pablo opening the door and complaining about the weather and glad to have us back. I gave a sigh of relief and both my companions gave nods of agreement. Not that we were safe; I had to remind myself that the stranger had walked through the wards and the walls without a problem.

People were rushing all through the building, some of them on fae business and others in the usual rush people get before the holidays.

Running out of time, I thought. We were all running out of time.

I still needed to brush up on my waltzing, too.

"I need to make a list," I said as we went up the stairs. Then I shook my head. "Or maybe not. If I had a list of all the things that needed to be done in the next couple days, it would be far too scary."

"True," Tessa agreed, which was not reassuring.

CHAPTER 7

About half way up to my apartment, we heard the laughter of children in one of the hallways. They were trying to sing carols, I thought, and I heard Rosa and Pat's voices as well. Happy people. My companions paused to listen. I had noticed that human children amazed them. Tessa had told me there were very few fae children, and to have so many kids in one place as both amazing and a bit frightening.

The sounds of the laughter put me in a better mood. Those were good, ordinary people without a bit of magic in them, and I'd help them have a better life. Rosa watched over the children during the day while Pam worked at Woo Woo News. She no longer had to take a job as a maid and her husband watched the entrance to the Fortress and kept my cars tuned. They were happy, especially after Rosa's brother Mateo and his kids moved into The Fortress as well. He was going to trade school, so having the kids right next door worked out well since Rosa was taking care of them. Mateo turned out to be an excellent carpenter and handyman. I planned to talk to him about starting his own business soon. I had already sent him to help my sister Violet with a broken water pipe. She liked his work and his attitude, and he seemed to get along with her. Someone who could get along with any of my sisters was bound to do well with others.

Pam was happy not only because she had someone she trusted watching the children, but also because she no longer had to worry about her soon to be Ex-Husband pounding on the door at all hours.

Jacobs was not happy about the new arrangement, either.

There were others who lived in the building, but I didn't see much of them. Anyone who didn't like the newcomers to the building had moved out.

I was happy to have done what I had for them, but as we reached the landing to my floor, I paused to look at my two companions, a new troubling thought coming to mind.

"I'm worried about all the trouble that seems to be piling up around me. I don't want it to affect the others here and upset the children."

"Ah." Brandis looked back down the stairs. "We must move carefully."

"As long the people who have been following us remain outside, we don't need to worry about them," Tessa said. He did not mention our guy walking through the wards. "We have too much going on right now. We'll be careful."

"Just get past the Winter Court," Brandis said and made it sound like an invocation. "We can deal with the humans after we settle with the fae."

I laughed slightly. I thought maybe my two friends didn't take the humans seriously enough, but right now I couldn't disagree. We had to prioritize and deal with the crazy fae before the crazy humans.

"I still need to come up with presents for my sisters. This is going to be difficult. I want something special this year and I am really out of time, which is my own fault."

"We'll help you find something," Tessa promised. "I think we can find something unique."

Oh, there was a thought. I felt better with the idea of Tessa's help.

At least I was staying fit with the fae around since we rarely used the elevator. I headed for the door to my apartment, glad to see refuge (as much as it was) in sight.

"If we survive the Winter Court, we'll be fine," Brandis said. "We can survive anything after that."

"You are not making me feel any better."

"I have mentioned that this isn't safe, right?" Tessa said with a little laugh. "We are already treading a dangerous line."

Tessa had explained to me that the situation was precarious and without parallel. Although all the fae in The Fortress -- with the exception of Vane -- took an oath to me as their Lord, they had not relinquished their Clan ties. Tessa was still the Cat Clan Totem. He would never change that, even if he could. Brandis and Kala were the war lords of their respective clans, but so long as they were here with me, my claim was the stronger. There were times when a single person might serve two clans, but never people of such standing as totems and war lords, and certainly never serving a human lord before.

"Once we send out the invitations, people can no longer ignore that we exist. They are going to have to make decisions, and that means change and commitment. While they may speak to the Queen of what they think, it is her decision that will be the final say. Some of them may decide to take us on before it goes that far, though so far they've all been quiet enough."

"I suspect the others don't realize how dangerous we are," Brandis added. We had reached the door.

"You're probably right," Tessa agreed. "There's also the problem of Gryn and Roan, who are no doubt spreading lies about us. The best we can do is to make this as perfect a Winter Court as we can manage. We are not weak in powers."

Tessa was right, of course. I supposed that people who thought the two clans held less power because they were too weak to come back to the fae lands were going to be in for a shock. Right now, the delay was mostly because of Vane, the Dragon Clan's shapeshifting totem who had been reborn -- well, re-hatched -- in this realm and hadn't recovered much of his true memory yet. Once he was stable --

I didn't want to think about that future.

I finally opened the door to my apartment and walked into a place where insanity seemed to rule. People from all three clans rushed around, notes flying through the air and landing on the table, a holographic map hanging near the wall with red spots glowing, and a dozen people talking at once.

"Ah good, Kala said as she stood up from the desk. "We need to practice waltzing, Summerfield. I am years out of practice."

"You better know now that we have another problem," Tessa announced. Everyone stopped and listened while he explained about the wish and magic.

Yes, that worried everyone.

Then we went back to work. I spent the afternoon practicing how to waltz with the Cat Clan Warlord while everyone else kept on being frantic and insane.

At least Kala appeared to be reasonably happy with my ability to waltz. I enjoyed gliding around the floor while everyone else did what work they could -- the kind of work I could not do, even if I did have a little touch of magic now. I wondered if Kala had been assigned to keep me entertained and out of everyone's way. Or maybe not -- after all, we did all have to worry about me stepping on the Queen of Fae's toes.

The weather had turned worse by late afternoon. No surprise there. Fierce winds blew against the windows, and I thought I could feel a little bit of a draft, which couldn't be good. The fae had the wards up. Nothing so mundane as a wind should have gotten through.

"That's not from us," Tessa said with a wave toward the balcony windows. Snow had begun to pile up on the ledge. "I don't sense any fae magic in the storm at all, but that doesn't mean it is natural."

"Our walk-through wards guy?" I asked.

"That would be my guess, especially after that show out on the street today. I'd like to up the power of the wards, but I'm sure it wouldn't help, and besides, the place would glow."

"Time to send people out to look around," Brandis said, and Kala nodded agreement. They glanced my way -- Lord Summerfield -- and I gave a nod as well. "I'll make certain they are all in pairs. I don't know if there is anything to be found, but we'd be stupid not to look."

The phone rang, and I noted it was Pablo from downstairs, which surprised me. I grabbed it up --

"Summerfield? Good. I have someone here," he said, and in Spanish, which he knew I understood. "He's from my old neighborhood. He has little English, but needs to tell you something. Can I bring him up?"

"Yes, thank you," I said, though my heart had started to thump a little harder. I put down the phone. "Pablo is bringing up someone who doesn't speak English and who has something to tell me. Maybe we'll get lucky, and it will be something for Woo Woo News."

"Ha," Tessa replied and dropped into a chair. "This is bound to be trouble."

Some of the others left at Brandis's orders, and all the obvious magic disappeared from the room. That would help. I couldn't begin to guess what kind of information someone from the Hispanic community might be bringing me, especially the part of that community where Pablo and his family had lived. This felt ... wrong.

I was the one who went and opened the door to let the two in, even though Brandis, Tessa, and Kala had all started to move that way. I recognized Pablo's companion. I'd met him last summer at the wake for one of their gang members. There had been a war when the Dragon Clan first arrived, but that trouble was over.

"Summerfield," he said with a nod. "I heard some odd news today. There are these men, gringos, nosing around the area and they are claiming you are a drug lord, and they want information on you --"

"Drug Lord," I repeated, stunned by the idea. "What the hell --"

The man gave a quick and emphatic nod. He had only come a little into the apartment, still mostly in the entry hall and shifted nervously. "They're not the problem, though. They're stupid, coming around and asking questions. But others -- bad people. They think you might be moving into their territory. They are making noises that maybe they need to be rid of you now."

I started to speak. Stopped. Tessa watched me from across the room and had probably picked up most of what had been said. Languages were not a problem for the fae. I was more than a little shocked by the news, and given the way things were going, that said a lot.

"Thank you." I started to reach for my billfold, but he stopped me with a touch on my arm. I could almost feel the fae all twitch at that moment.

"No, Summerfield. No. We know who paid to have the house rebuilt the house that burnt down last month. We know who paid the bills when little Marco was hit by a car. No."

I hadn't thought any of them knew. I started to say something more, but he patted my arm and stepped outside the door. Pablo paused, though.

"You take this serious, yes?" he said and in English this time. "These are dangerous people. They are serious."

"I will, Pablo," I promised. "You take care, too. They may know you work here. Are things all right with you? Your wife and kids are doing all right here?"

"You joke, yes?" he said with a slight laugh. "We would not do well here? This is paradise, Summerfield."

"It might not be safe here, though. You might want to go somewhere else, at least for a while. I can arrange --"

"I will not abandon you," he replied. I felt another of those odd rushes of power.

"Think about your children --"

"They are safer now than they have ever been. You take

care."

He headed out to gather up his unnamed companion in the hall. I closed the door wondering how this mess had gotten started. Then I went back to the table and sat down.

"The people watching this place, is that part of this trouble?" Kala asked.

"They might be," Tessa agreed. He went out on the balcony, untouched by the wind and unseen by anyone down there on the street. Beyond the magical shell, the wind blew more fiercely, and I had a sense of menace and trouble in the air. Tessa stared out for a few minutes, then nodded and came back in. "He's gone. Driving a big four-wheel truck with a scoop, too. I don't think he'll have trouble getting home."

"I can't believe we have even more trouble," I mumbled.

"This is human trouble, but serious enough," Tessa said. I supposed that some of the others might dismiss it because of the human element.

I left him to talk to the others who wandered in and out. I went to my computer and began checking to make certain all our paperwork was up to date and that we were looking legit. I did it mostly just to keep busy and focused on something until I could get better control of my anger. The idea that anyone accused me of dealing drugs had caused a bad reaction, and I didn't want to do anything that might include magic, and that I would no doubt regret.

Things were getting out of hand.

The wind blew harder again.

CHAPTER 8

When I finally felt as though I could think clearly, I moved away from the desk and out to the kitchen. Stocked up with tea and cookies, I headed to the table and waved the others to sit down as well.

"We need to think this through," I said. "We know we're being watched and followed. If those people are from the drug cartel, then they can be extremely dangerous."

The other three nodded. Everyone but Tessa, Brandis and Kala had left, and I appreciated the nice, quiet gathering. Except for York and Vane, the others still often got too worried around me.

We need to find out who is spreading these lies about you," Tessa announced with a bit of a snarl in his voice.

"Don't take this too personally," I replied and reminded myself to do the same. "This could be someone trying to upset my family. It could also be one of my cousins. There are some of them who would be thrilled to see me in trouble, and who have just enough income to make this kind of trouble for the fun of it."

They had not considered those possibilities and it seemed to have settled them a little better. I even hoped it was true. We talked through a little bit more, but York arrived, and he looked ... well, he looked pleased until we told him the latest news.

"That's insane," York said and sounded annoyed for the first time since I'd met him. Then he waved the words off. "We have other things. The Ice Palace is ready to see."

"Don't you people ever sleep?" I asked, shocked by the news.

"Not often these days," Tessa admitted as he stood. "And we aren't likely to until the Winter Court is over. I forgot to tell you that we made the portal and located the spot for the palace, didn't I?"

"You need to check it over," York said. "You need to see the place and give your okay before we send out the invitations."

I almost simply waved it off and said I trusted them, but I saw something hopeful in York's face just then. They'd been working hard on this, and I needed to show my appreciation for the work and not just the trust I had in them.

"When do we go?" I asked.

"Now is a good time," Tessa decided and stood. "Let us go see this wonder and get the invitations out. We are running out of time."

I glanced out the window. Sunset had arrived in a glory of red and gold as the storm clouds parted. The snow was little more than a fine mist in the air. Once those clouds slipped away, the night would turn bitterly cold.

So, I headed for an Ice Palace. That might even make sense in the way my life worked these days.

We went down the stairs and into the garage where carpenters had left their tools. I had meant to come down earlier and see how they were doing and to thank them for the work. I had never ignored people working for me, but it seemed that since I took the role of Lord Summerfield, that it was far more important.

They were building a castle as a surprise for the kids who needed a play area inside The Fortress this winter. I was already negotiating for the old building behind us, which I would turn into a garage and more apartments, with a covered walkway over the alley between the two buildings.

Right now, the castle masked something else. I ducked through the entrance and followed Tessa to the far back of The Fortress wall and past a pretend wall made of magic that hid what was only four feet beyond it. As we stepped through, I found myself looking at a wide, glowing tunnel of light.

The hair on my arms stood up as I stared into an area that seemed to go on forever. Then I thought about the amount of power it had to take to fuel this magic, and I turned to Tessa with real worry.

"How can you keep this going?" I asked, and the words seemed to echo out ahead of us into the light.

"Probably the best thing about your realm is that there is power to spare here and very few who can use it." He stepped into the tunnel, and I went with him. Trusting I suppose. "I just had to create the tunnel and then set the spell to fuel it. The magic takes little upkeep."

I had never dealt with anything so magical before unless you count the fae themselves. The tunnel seemed to be made of braided rainbows of vibrant, beautiful colors. I wasn't surprised because I had never seen the fae make anything that was ugly.

"How far does this go?" I asked, staring into the light.

"We'll only go a few more steps," Brandis said as he moved up ahead of us, reminding me that I did need guards now. "You have to keep the entrance and the exit a few yards apart, or they can get muddled and then there's no telling where you might end up."

The floor felt oddly slick, like walking on glass, but without the fear of sliding. My skin tingled, but we really didn't have far to go. Brandis had already stepped out of the light into a hall of blue ice. Pretty, and not nearly as cold as I had expected, but that was probably fae magic again. The ice hall wasn't long, and we stepped out into --

Magic.

That was all I could think as I looked around. The walls glowed with hints of rainbows. Creatures of ice and stood atop shimmering columns. Looking higher, I thought the fae had captured stars and put them in the ceiling, and that gave the building a glow. The main room was cavernous, with other halls every few yards, and at the far end of the room stood a throne of stars and ice sat atop a series of steps.

"This -- this is gorgeous," I said, shocked, amazed, and very pleased.

Those halls lead to areas for each of the other Clans," York explained with a wave of his hand towards the halls that radiated out of the main room. Above each, I saw the carved emblem of each clan, plus an extra one that had to be for the Queen and her court. That one glowed with rainbow colors, shifting across an emblem of a tree and sky. I looked over my shoulder and found a globe of ice, spinning amid a field of stars. Nice.

"You have outdone yourselves," Tessa said with a bright smile. That he looked so shocked and amazed made me realize this was extraordinary even by fae standards.

"They will not find our lord wanting in anything, including elegance," York replied and with more emotion than I was used to seeing in him.

York was taking this very seriously, but I saw the same look in the others. They all nodded, and I realized they were putting on a show of pride, and they were not going to let anyone think they were poorer for having a non-fae clan leader. I just had to do my best not to embarrass them.

The pixies had shown up at my feet, but now they rushed out into the ice palace, laughing with delight. Soon they were climbing walls and sliding back down them and across the floor. Everyone looked amused.

"I can't remember so grand a hall for the Winter Palace," Tessa said and clearly meant those words.

"The last ones I attended were all in dull places," Brands said with a sneer of distaste I had not seen in him before. "Old palaces, barely fixed up for the event. Lackluster music. Everyone retired early just to get out of there. Oh yes, we are going to surprise people this year."

"And annoy them?" I asked, worried for new reasons.

"Some," Tessa admitted. He smiled. "Gryn and Roan are going to be upset. Should we let that bother us?"

I laughed. Maybe this would be fun after all.

"I have only known little magics, you know," I reminded them, looking at York, Brandis, and Tessa. "I hadn't considered the full wonder of what you can do."

"Sometimes we even amaze ourselves," Tessa admitted.

We took a tour of the room. One area had an alcove with tables and food already there.

"We ordered food from a lot of different places in Omaha," Tessa said with a nod at the tables. The scents were enticing. "I did my best not to clear out any single place. I am still amazed at the plethora of human foods that are so readily acquired. We keep them fresh with magic. You will be getting the bills for the orders."

I laughed again, delighted. Lightheaded, most likely. Until now, I had worried that we couldn't pull this off.

"I would like permission to broadcast the invitation and open the link," York said. "That will alert the others that this is going to happen. I'm sure they're almost as anxious as we are by now. Some of us will stay here and help them get settled as they arrive."

"Should I remain as well?" I asked.

"No," Tessa said with a nod to the hall that headed back to The Fortress. "The Lord who is holding the Court does not arrive until Queen Amata does, and she won't be here early. That's good because we do still have more work back at The Fortress.

"Then send the message," I said to York, even though the idea still bothered me.

"We'll take care of things here," York assured me. I had the feeling he was the one in charge and that he might even be enjoying the work. I had always thought of York as shy and retiring, but maybe he only needed the right job. He had done excellent work here.

"You will be careful." I put a hand on York's arm. "I know there are rules, and this should be neutral territory, but since I am involved, there may be those who believe that the rules do not apply in this case. All of you remain careful. I don't want to lose any of my friends."

I won nods from all around, and then Tessa and Brandis led me back to our hall. Tessa stopped there, though, and looked back at the room.

"This is going to be glorious." He had one of his Cheshire Cat smiles.

We went back through the portal with the pixies rushing to join us. They disappeared again when we stepped into the garage, and I feared they might like being invisible a little too much. They did play pranks now and then, but never anything too serious. I'd let them have their fun for now, though I thought I should probably sit down and have a talk with them about behaving at the Winter Court --

"The pixies," I said. "What do we do about them?"

"Then won't attend the Winter Court itself. If they did, every pixie in every clan would suddenly align with Queen Amata," Tessa explained. "They stay clear of it -- their own choice in this case. In fact, during the entire time of the Winter Court, we aren't likely to see them. They have their own gathering, though no one is quite certain where."

"Good," I replied. "One problem I don't have to worry about in this mess."

We were barely five steps past the portal when my phone began to ring: Yellow Rose of Texas. I wondered what my sister wanted.

"Hello?" I said with a bit more of a tentative sound than I liked.

She didn't notice. "There you are! Where have you been?

I've been trying to reach you for the last hour! Never mind, just listen. We have a problem. The place where we normally hold the Holiday gathering lost most of the roof in the storm last night. I'm hunting for somewhere else, but you know how hard it will be to find any kind of place this late --"

Oh yes, I understood that very well.

Tessa put a hand on my arm while she prattled on about all the places that were *not* available. "Here," he said softly. "We can make it work."

I looked at him, panicked at the idea. The only place big enough would be the garage, and it was not the sort of setting my extraordinarily rich family was used to.

"Sunflower, are you listening to me?" Rose demanded.

"Almost. Hold on. I may have an answer."

She made an exasperated sound. I hit mute so she wouldn't hear the insanity on my end.

"We cannot possibly hold it here, Tessa. This is the only area large enough and --

He smiled and gave a wave of his hand. The garage changed into a huge, lovely room with wooden walls, carpeted floor, chandeliers --

"Ah."

He nodded and wiped everything away with another wave of his hand. "We'll do as much as we can without magic, but we can make it work with magic if we need to."

I took a deep breath and took the mute off. "Rose? Are you still there?" I asked.

"Of course, I'm still here. I'll get back to you --"

"We can have it here, Rose," I said and tried hard not to sound panicked at the idea.

"You. There." She sounded as though she might be choking. "Sunflower --"

"I can do this. I will hire the people to get right on it. Trust me."

She made more sounds. Then she sighed. "Oh God. I really don't have a choice. I've tried everywhere --"

"Thank for the vote of confidence, Rose."

"I'll --" She stopped. Took another breath. "I'll start calling the others. Good luck. Bye."

She hung up before I could say anything more. I stared at the phone for a moment before I put it away. "This had better work, Tessa. You really don't want to annoy my sisters."

"This is no worse than the Winter Court," he said. I wasn't so sure. "We can do this one, too."

"I'll get a list of everything they've already lined up," I said. Like I needed more work. "My grandparents have a favorite chef, too. We'll use him for the main meal. We'll need to build a kitchen, and it is going to have to be top grade. I think there is also a quintet or some such that has been engaged. There will be about three hundred people, including several children. We'll need a Christmas Tree. And I still haven't found presents for my sisters."

"We can make this work," Brandis said with a surprisingly bright smile. "It is simply one more addition to the insanity, and we're handling that fine already."

The insanity part I had to agree with so I might as well go along with the rest of it. I looked around the garage and tried to remember the vision that Tessa had presented as a lure to draw me in.

If this didn't work, we were all going to be in a lot of

trouble.

I headed upstairs to practice waltzing.

CHAPTER 9

I had been planning for a nice, quiet holiday. I thought I might even slip out of town before the first and visit Glynis and her parents. She'd been hinting at it in the texts I got. She knew, with my family gathering coming up, that I would be busy -- but she didn't know the half of it.

I had spent several hours learning something that had bothered me, but I hadn't decided how to approach the question. Kala was the one who brought it up as we rested after waltzing again.

"There are five major clans: Wolf, Eagle, Centaur, Cat, and Dragon," she said. "We have become what is known as an Associative Clan. They form now and then from various groupings of other clans and usually for some specific trouble that needs worked out."

"Ah." I nibbled on some crackers and cheese. "And after the trouble?"

"Sometimes they disband," Brandis said as he sat down at the table with us. "Sometimes, they don't. Eagle Clan was an Associative called Sky Clan back then -- but a new totem appeared, and they became Eagle Clan."

"Some Associative Clans stay together for hundreds of years," Kala added. She blinked and shook her head. I suspected she had thought about me and the passage of time, but I didn't ask. "I have belonged to two in the past. They do not sever your tie to your original clan, but for a time you are called to a higher duty because of a higher need."

"And the higher need that brought you together with me?" I asked.

"Protecting your world," Brandis said.

He had a good point.

Later I stood out in the inevitable snowstorm with fae guards -- most of them invisible -- every few feet between me and the street.

Tessa had spent the morning doing readings. None of them had looked particularly bad, but there had always been a little hint of trouble coming.

We waited for the delivery guy to get done taking in all the cooking and refrigeration equipment and putting it into the new room we'd created out of a lower-level storage area. I had gotten a list of what Chef Kendrew considered the best equipment and simply ordered it in and paid for the quick delivery and installation. I had begun to think that having an in-building cafe wasn't a bad idea anyway. Most of my people didn't keep regular schedules.

We were going to do as much work on the 'ballroom' without magic as we could manage so that we didn't have to worry about failures or mishaps there. While Tessa had used magic to put things together, he'd used real wood, nails, and other items as much as he could rather than rely on illusion. This also meant that I had to handle things like deliveries and questions from others. I was beginning to think my fae companions were simply trying to keep me busy.

It was working.

It didn't help that my sisters had started calling every few minutes. All five of them, one after another, like they had a schedule they were keeping. I had considered turning off the phone, except that I needed it to keep in touch with people who were still making deliveries, despite the weather and the late date.

Then, to make my day even better, Ted Jacobs showed up. Jacobs was not my favorite person and the way he swaggered up to the walkway, holding a couple wrapped boxes, made me want to tell him to go to hell.

However, I didn't have the right to make that call right now.

"Pablo, can you call Pam and ask if she wants to see Ted?" I asked, looking back to the doorway where Pablo stood, watching Ted with obvious distaste of his own.

Pablo gave a nod and stepped inside.

"I got a right --" Ted began.

I lifted a hand, and Tessa took a step closer. Jacob's stopped moving, and his shifting eyes showed his true worry.

"Pam will let us know if she wants to see you. If not, you can take it up with your lawyer, though you've seen how well that does already."

He snarled, but he didn't argue. There was something so furtive about his movements and glances that I would just as soon have run him off the property.

"Pam says to come up, no more than fifteen minutes," Pablo said. He held the phone. "I will time it from when she says you are there, and if you do not leave when she says, others will deal with removing you."

Pablo had said it all so clearly that I didn't see any reason to add more. Jacob skittered past us and into the building. I watched him go with such complete and utter distrust, that Tessa must have felt the emotion. He looked uneasy as well. He made a little hiss of a sound -- cat-like right then.

He sighed. "I don't like him."

"Neither do I, but he's not worth making trouble over right now. We have far too many other problems to work on."

"True," Tessa agreed. Kala came out of the snow to the right, appearing as she neared. She frowned too, but I didn't think it had anything to do with Jacobs.

"The people in the van are back," she said. "Not far away and really interested in what's going on here."

"Leave them alone," I said. "We don't want to antagonize someone into actions we are going to dislike."

She looked glum at the answer, but then she was the Cat Clan's Warlord and probably wanted to use her powers. "They can't hear us anyway. Looks like the delivery is done. I'll go off and help York."

"Thank you," I said.

She smiled brightly this time. "Eagle Clan has arrived," she said, which was the first news I'd had of what was going on in the wilds of the arctic circle. "And yes, they were impressed."

"Really?" Tessa replied with an eyebrow raised. "It has always been hard to get any reaction out of them."

"We are doing well," Kala said and sounded about as surprised as I felt.

The delivery people were done, and I tipped them all. Then a van load of men arrived and filed out, heading my way.

I almost panicked, but Pablo came out and patted me on the shoulder.

"You say you need people to set up this kitchen. Here they are. They do good work."

"Excellent!" I had put Pablo to the task of finding some help for us.

"They come from the old neighborhood, many of them," he admitted. I had already realized that part. "Know the work, though. I will show them and get them started."

My phone rang. Aster this time. I sighed and keyed it on.

"I have everything under control," I said before she could even speak.

"I thought of something, SB," she said, sounding almost as frantic as Rose. "Children. There are going to be children at the gathering --"

"I have already taken that into account," I assured her.

"We have presents for them," she said as though she had not even heard me. "But they need to be entertained. I was there once when they weren't, and it wasn't fun. And worse, they are mostly spoiled."

She had a point. I'd been to those gatherings, too, and remembered how annoying it had been to have a bunch of spoiled brats constantly begging for attention. I started to get worried -- but Tessa shook his head. He held out his hand and on it a small bear danced.

"Magic," he said with a smile.

Oh, excellent answer. "I have it covered, Aster," I said and with such assurance that she made a little hiss of surprise.

"Okay," she said and didn't sound as reassured as I had hoped. However, she did hang up without bothering me about anything more.

I put the phone away and shook my head. "I know they aren't used to me taking care of things, but I wish they --"

Tessa tackled me and knocked me straight down into the snow.

"What the hell --" I started. Then I realized what I had done. "Ah. The wish thing."

"Yes," he said.

"You can get up now. It's safe."

"You need to be careful. Too much depends on what's going on, and we don't care let you be careless, Summerfield."

"Yeah. Sorry." We got up as Ted came out of the building, and he stopped to smirk at us.

"Is there something you want?" I asked, and half-wished, though silently, that I could take a swing at him right then.

"I'll be seeing you in court, Sunflower," he said and purposely shouldered his way past the two of us.

He fell on the ice about four steps further. I couldn't even tell if it had been the work of any of my people or not. Sometimes Karma takes care of things, which was a good reminder to me not to get belligerent even towards Jacobs. I did laugh.

He scrambled back to his feet, muttered several curses, and headed on down the street, soon lost in the fall of snow. Just as well. I didn't need that kind of provocation today. Tessa still frowned, though.

"He is in for a real shock when Rose gets hold of him in court," I said with a bright smile. "I am looking forward to it."

"He's trouble," Tessa said and got that look he had when a vision came to him. I held my breath. We had far too much going on already. Tessa shook his head. "I can't tell what is going to happen. Just trouble everywhere."

"I don't need you to feed my paranoia."

The phone rang. I dealt with Chef Kendrew again who seemed on the flighty side. I supposed artistic types were more apt to panic, but I reassured him that everything was going well. I think he even believed me again, but I couldn't say it would hold for long.

We went inside and started for the stairs -- and our *walks through walls* guy appeared again. Tessa lifted a hand out of habit, but I stepped in front of him. This stranger was not someone who would take well to even a hint of a threat.

He was larger than life, though not in a huge, towering sort of way. Rather it came as the *feel* he projected. His hair was too perfectly curled, as was his beard -- both of which were completely out of place in the modern world. His dark eyes stared at me without blinking; his lips pulled into a frown.

He wore the pants and shirt well, but I could tell he was not comfortable in them. I had known others from the desert lands who felt the same way, which again convinced me that he was from the Near East -- just not the *modern* Near East.

"You are not what you seem," he said, his voice echoing oddly in the little area -- larger than life again.

"True. But that does not mean I am a problem for you," I replied while I fought against the urge to bow my head. This one was power incarnate, even if he tried to hide that in a human form. The question was which power?

"You have claimed my domain, human."

"Are you a fae lord?" I dared to ask.

"Fae?" This word was clearly not a term he understood.

Tessa shifted nervously, and Brandis arrived, but I signaled him to stay back.

"I mean you no harm. Whatever I have done was unintentional."

He leaned towards me. I did not back up, even though I thought we might all die right there. We faced something far beyond fae magic, and I knew that showing weakness would lead to defeat and we would not survive that, either.

"If you mean me no harm, then give up your hold on the world," he ordered.

The world and not *his* world. I found that choice of wording interesting, though not particularly helpful right now.

"I can't. Others would suffer if I renounced what I now am," I said. He pulled back, frowning. "Even so, I still mean you no harm."

The more I watched him, the more I thought I should know who he was, which was very strange. I was dealing with a very ancient power, and I wanted a clue on how to handle him. He was an unknown, and probably the worst trouble of all.

"You do this for them," he said with a wave of his hand towards my two companions. I had the feeling that others were gathering, but I didn't dare try to warn them away. "You hold on to the power to keep them safe, and yet they are not human."

"Neither are you."

He blinked but didn't deny my words. "I have always had a link to humans. But these are newcomers with little powers."

"Nevertheless, they are in my care." I decided that I might as well be straightforward in this one. "Why are you here?"

He blinked, and his eyes narrowed. Did he not know why he was here? That wasn't going to help much.

"I slept, but you awoke me, however briefly," he said. His head tilted and some of the anger left his face. "Then I slept a little while again and heard you speak the words of power and claim the world. I had not expected this from you. You were not born to the power."

"I understand the danger," I said and tried to sound as though I believed those words. "Still, I will not let others suffer for what I lack in understanding. I am doing my best to learn."

He took a step backward, and while he still frowned, he did not look quite as angry. I took that as a win.

"I will watch," he said. He stared at me, but he was aware of the others, too. I knew when Brandis moved and hoped he didn't do anything brash. I didn't want to lose any of my friends to this new madness. "I will watch and wait. What you do affects the world, Summerfield."

I didn't like that he knew my name and I didn't know his. I saw him tilt his head as though waiting, but I didn't ask. I knew that if I did, I was admitting to a weakness. Names were important.

"Judge your actions," he said, his voice softer. "Judge your thoughts. I watch."

He took another step back and left the building as a warm breeze from somewhere else circled us. A bit of sand fell to the floor.

"Well, like I don't have paranoia enough already," I said with a sigh. I looked to see a dozen fae behind me. My friends had arrived when I was in danger, but that simply made this worse. "Any idea about what we're facing here?"

"Not a clue," Tessa admitted. Brandis merely frowned and stared at the sand as though he expected it to get up and do something. Okay, I had stared as well. "I don't like that he thinks the fae are new to this, though. I don't know if he doesn't realize we're from somewhere else and only new to this realm, or if he is judging us based on his own existence which would mean --"

"He's very, very ancient," I said. "I'm sure of that part."

"He has the feel of an old power," Brandis agreed. We finally headed for the stairs. Kala had knelt and gathered up the sand. "I will still try to speak to Arinith. He might have a better idea of what this guy is and what we should do. We'll see him at the Winter Court if not before."

"Maybe we awakened him when we took our oaths to you," Tessa suggested. "there was a hellish amount of power around with Arinith involved. I'll see if I can trace anything unusual happening then. Meanwhile, you need to go practice waltzing with Kala."

Sad to say, those words didn't even sound odd to me.

CHAPTER 10

I was completely exhausted by the time I crawled into bed. The clock said a little after two in the morning. I started to close my eyes and then remembered that we would be starting the Winter Court by this time tomorrow. Maybe I shouldn't sleep after all. Maybe I should never sleep again.

Presents for my sisters. I had forgotten that part again. Maybe I could give them all a trip to the Bahamas and ship them out of my life for a few weeks. That appealed to me, though it did nothing for the current crisis. The real problems hadn't even begun yet, and I already couldn't think straight.

Or sleep.

Maybe I shouldn't waste time on sleep. I could --

I began to slip away and straight into a dream.

I found myself in a familiar place; a place I had known when I was a kid. That made it difficult because we'd traveled so much when I was younger that the places had blurred together in my mind. In the dream, I stood on a hill --

No, not a hill. A tell. Beneath me lay an ancient city, unexplored yet by archaeologists. I could see potsherds embedded in the sandy surface, and I picked one up for my collection. I was -- not in Egypt. I knew this, in the oddly logical way that we do in our dreams. Not Israel, either.

Somewhere farther to the east?

The night fell in my dream, a diamond tiara of stars brightening the sky above me. Being alone in odd places and wandering around didn't bother me. I knew to watch for snakes and scorpions as well as whatever other dangerous creatures might find a young boy being less careful than was wise. I had grown up in many dangerous places. I was careful.

I could hear the sounds from the camp down the far side of the tell. The locals were singing and playing music. My parents and the teacher would be by the fire, sharing food. They'd save some for me. They always did because I usually went exploring when the sun started to go down and the day grew cooler.

The tell rose a little behind me still with a sharp, narrow cliff up at the top. I decided to go on and reach the summit. I could see clearly by the rising moon. Bits of pots showed here and there, as well as the shape of ancient sun-dried bricks. I wondered which forgotten city this might be.

The climb was not difficult. Sometimes I thought back to the times we'd spent in Nepal and those areas, and the hikes I had made with Sherpas, either with my parents or without them. Those had been real climbs -- though I admitted that I didn't mind being somewhere not so cold. I thought I felt a chill wind tonight (though was that part of the dream or the knowledge of snow outside my Omaha window?). I hurried to the top, scraping my palm when I slipped slightly, but nothing worse.

From the top, I could see the remote village and a little walk showed the fire down below, and the people gathered here. That looked far more inviting than being alone now that

I'd completed my quest to reach the top. I scrambled around on the top of the tell, seeing what I could find without digging, which was forbidden. I exchanged one sherd for another and finally decided that my blankets would be nicer than sitting in the dirt.

I knew enough to be careful going down the side of the tell. I couldn't clearly see the path I had taken up, but the area had been mostly clear, so I started down. Slowly, of course. I knew not to move too quickly and to test out my footing --

And I still fell through into a hole.

It wasn't a far fall, but I landed on my back with the air knocked out of me. Dirt began to fall in where I'd come through, and I rolled away, afraid that the falling debris would bury me. However, the collapse stopped. I could clearly see the opening, not too far away. If nothing else, I could yell until someone found me. I didn't want to do that, though.

The moonlight glinted across the opening, and I could see pots sitting on shelves. Sitting there, whole and untouched. Bricks lined the walls, a hint of color where the light touched them. I was in a room -- a long, narrow room, with shelves and at the end, straight across from me, was a statue.

I stood and moved closer. I didn't recognize any of the symbols, though I understood that the little statues around him were symbols for worshippers. Their huge eyes looked dark and forbidding, and I knew that I had intruded. But I went past them and touched the arm of the statue.

"Sorry," I whispered with a bow of my head.

Then I climbed the statue, balanced on his head and reached for the opening not far above. I caught hold and pulled myself up out of the hole. Things shifted again, and I scrambled away as dirt fell in and rocks slid down, covering the opening. What I had found by accident was hidden from the world again.

I had an odd feeling that the statue wanted it that way. I didn't tell my parents about my adventure. It was my secret place.

I awoke to the scent of cinnamon rolls and tea, but the memory of the dream drove me out of bed and grabbing my robe. I quickly headed out into the other room without considering how seeing me fresh from bed was affect the others. They watched me, stunned and silent as I stumbled past them to the desk on the far wall.

I began ravaging my way through the drawers. "Paper. Pencil," I mumbled. Too long in the digital world -- I couldn't find anything, and I grew increasingly annoyed.

"Here you go Lord Summerfield, sir," Tessa said and put a tablet and pencil before me.

His tone had been so perfectly Jeeves-like that he made me laugh, which helped. I quickly sketched out the symbols I had seen in the room, however imperfectly. After a few lines and slashes, I knew what they were, but not what they said.

"Cuneiform," I said with a frown. "An ancient writing system. I must have fallen into a temple."

"Temple?" Tessa said.

I told them about the dream and how I was certain it was a clear memory from my earlier life, and how certain I was this was related to our visitor. "I sensed he was from the Near East. I can probably decipher stuff, given time. We don't have any right now, but I might figure it out later if we need to."

Tessa nodded. "We do seem to be lacking in time at the

moment."

"I'll go shower and dress. The food smells great."

The lines cuneiform danced through my head for the rest of the morning. I even went to a cabinet in the living room and drew out a sherd. It had a date on the card it sat on, as well as a location, which was somewhere in Iraq. I wondered if anyone else had investigated the tell. I thought not since the temple, so clearly untouched by time and thieves, would have been news. I had been the first -- and last -- to stand there for thousands of years.

I shivered wondering what I had touched ... what I had briefly awakened and then called back again when I became the Lord of the Earth.

CHAPTER 11

I pulled at the collar of my suit jacket, though not because it didn't fit. Kala and York had made certain that the suit would fit perfectly, and I'd never worn anything so comfortable before in my life. No, the show of unease had a different reason. We were standing outside the tunnel, waiting for Tessa to signal us to come through. He was tracking the Fae Queen and her entourage, and we had to time my arrival as close as possible.

I felt as though I was heading to my prom with a blind date.

Which I had never done, of course -- never attended a prom. For that matter, I had never dated until Glynis. I'd written a quick note to her earlier and said it was looking crazy on this end and not to be surprised if I was slow to answer her for a while.

I had wondered, sometimes, what it would have been like to do all the normal teen things that even my sisters suffered through, but I had missed. I should not have even considered it. Karma has a knack for listening to those unwise whispers.

The others around me were remarkably calm. I thought this was remarkable considering that York had sent word, so we knew now that Gryn was there with Roan and several of the Centaur Clan. I don't think Tessa was the only one who growled at the news, but they were all calmer now.

Vane was with us, though not in the Summerfield colors, of course. He had chosen to go in with us rather than stay with those members of his clan not associated with me. Brandis and York were with me, of course, and so were many Cat Clan people.

"That's the sign," Brandis said as a light flashed in the tunnel. "Are you ready?"

"What an interesting question," I said as we started forward. "I wonder how I should answer it. I think the best way might be to say that I could not possibly ever be ready for this."

The others laughed, and we came out of the magic tunnel in good cheer, at least. We didn't slow, and in a few steps, I was out into a hall filled with far too many fae. I'm not certain how I kept moving. The feel of the place was overwhelming. Colors and lights danced over the walls and the banners of the clans hung on the wall over the throne -- including mine in the middle.

The fae had gathered in groups according to their clan so that spots of various colors stood near the walls: The grays of Wolf Clan, Blue of Eagles Clan, Red of Centaur Clan, Black of Cat Clan, Brown of Dragon Clan (those that were not oathed to me for the last two), and the Green of Summerfield Clan. Brandis had pointed out that it was easy to tell what clans were aligned by how they mingled.

Fae looked towards us, more than a little surprised, I thought, to see the group who accompanied me. Vane had to be a surprise, since he had no ties to me, except in friendship and that I had stood the square and helped protect him when he'd hatched.

The Queen arrived in a flurry of blue lights and a breeze that hinted at snow and ice; fresh and clean and filled with the power of every storm that ever spread across a winter land. Tall, stately -- she had hair the color of trees denuded of leaves and eyes the shade of ice on a pond. I bowed with everyone else, knowing she looked my way and wondered if I would survive for another heartbeat.

I did. And another after that one.

Tessa touched my arm. We were about to face our first test. Tessa, the Totem of the Cat Clan, would introduce me. If she disapproved --

Prince Arinith cut between us and waved Tessa aside. Then he took me the rest of the way to meet the Queen, and yes that was noted by everyone. Though he didn't wear our colors, Arinith had taken an oath to me, and this was someone so powerful that normally he would never belong to any clan. I had tried to release him from his oath, but he hadn't responded, and this was the first I'd seen him since last fall right after he took his place in my clan.

"My Queen," Arinith said with a bow of his head. "I am pleased to introduce you to my Lord Summerfield."

I suppose if you are going to go for the show, you might as well go all the way. I bowed my head with a slight sideways glance to see a quirk of his lips. Oh yes, Prince Arinith was enjoying the display. Queen Amata appeared amused, but I was far from certain that meant anything good for me.

"Summerfield," she said, which was an admission that she acknowledged my place, at least for the moment. "It is unprecedented that a High Elf should introduce anyone to me."

Her voice sounded like a soft breeze that came before a sudden storm, and like music too exquisite to understand. I wondered if it affected others the way it did me -- I had no inherent protections against magic, after all. I took a breath and looked up at last. She was beautiful, of course. I would expect nothing less from a Fae Queen. But I had expected something dire in the stare she gave me, rather than the open curiosity.

"I fear, Queen Amata, that everything I do will be unprecedented. How can it not be? However, I mean no disrespect to you or the rest of the fae realm. I never planned to take this position."

She gave me a pensive glance, and I held my breath. If she decided now, then the matter was closed -- and I could not see how she could decide in my favor. I could only hope that being here, in connection with the rest of the fae, would give my people a chance to return to their clans and not be in danger, even if they did lose power.

"Would you step down?" she asked suddenly.

Asked, not commanded. I took a breath and decided to be daring. "Can you promise the safety of my people if I did so?" I asked.

Her head tilted slightly. "Well asked. Perhaps we will discuss the matter again, later."

So, Clan Summerfield survived for a while longer. I gave her a bow of thanks.

She turned to the others who had been almost as nervous about what was going on as I had felt. I could see it in the faces of all the rest of the fae here. I don't know what they wanted or expected, but they looked relieved to have her raise her hands, a sprinkling of magic stars flying through the air.

"Welcome to the Winter Court," she said, her voice bright and cheerful. "Let the festivities begin!"

She gave me another curious look, but I knew this part. It was time to waltz with the Fae Queen.

"I am honored to offer the first dance, Queen Amata," I said and bowed again.

York had prepped the orchestra to play a favorite of the Queen's -- a human song, as it happened, so one that had never been played at a court function before. *Invitation to the Waltz* by Weber starts out slow and builds. We had a few slow turns to get the feel of each other before the music grew as wild as a summer storm. We managed the dance, and in the end, I bowed, and she laughed with delight. I couldn't say I'd made any more friends for having done so well, but it was delightful to see how happy the dance had made her.

"Well done," Prince Arinith said as he passed me and disappeared into the crowd following the Queen toward her throne.

"Excellent!" Tessa added with a slap on my shoulder. And yes, that drew attention, too.

Some of the lords and ladies were standing off in a show of aloofness, if not disdain, while Queen Amata remained uncertain about my future as the Lord of Earth. That was all right; they could keep their distance. I was not going to pretend to be one of them, and if they did nothing more than look annoyed, I didn't care.

I wandered through the large room with Tessa and Brandis at my back. I suspected my two unusual guards would mark those they thought might be more trouble, but for the moment, the first day of the Winter Court seemed to be going well.

"Tessa," a woman said close by. I heard a hint of love and loss in the name.

"Lady Ethna." Tessa bowed his head and then reached out and embraced the woman. "Lord Summerfield, this is Lady Ethna, the leader of the Cat Clan. I am so glad to see you here, Lady."

"I am happy to see you again after so long," she said with a hand on Tessa's arm. "You have been parted from your clan for too long, my friend."

Her eyes flickered my way with a little distrust, but that passed. My association with Tessa was only a few months long, while Tessa and some of the other Cat Clan members had remained trapped in my realm for centuries. They'd never really told me how long, but I was under the impression that the Industrial Revolution had barely gotten off the ground when Gryn tricked them.

I didn't want to show anger here, though I had no doubt she already mistrusted me since I held her Clan Totem in my service. Oh, and Kala, her Cat Clan Warlord, as well.

Kala had crossed back to join us after a discussion with someone else. She did not bow to the woman, though. Instead, she embraced her.

"Mother," she said, startling me.

"Kala, my love. I'll ask now: will you come back home with us? Will all of you, so that the sundered part of the clan, can return to their true home?"

Her eyes turned to me, not to them.

"They have always known they have the right to do what they think best. I will do nothing to hold any of the others back if they wish to return to their home."

She gave me a more gracious nod. I was aware that others listened, a circle of silence spreading around my little group. Brandis looked bothered, but I wasn't certain if that was because he had to make decisions about going home or if he worried that the Cat Clan would desert us.

"I cannot return yet, Lady," Tessa was the one who spoke. "There are visions I have seen. Gryn --"

"Prince Arinith brought us the news about Gryn himself," she said and cast a glare to the side, over my right shoulder. I felt a chill, thinking of him back there somewhere. I didn't need to worry, though, with Tessa and Brandis as my guards. And Kala, of course. She stood at her mother's shoulder now and was not going to let anything happen. "Oh yes, I can see how you must settle such things before you come back home. But you will someday?"

"Oh yes," Tessa said and grinned brightly. "I thought I might bring Lord Summerfield for a visit. He is in sore need of finding out what the dignity of being a fae clan leader means."

She stared at him, aghast at such words -- until I laughed. "He's right, you know."

She laughed as well and the others with her. Lady Ethna put a hand on my arm. Brandis gave a little twitch, the reaction of the Dragon Clan Warlord to the leader of a clan who had been his enemy for longer than I could imagine. She raised an eyebrow.

He bowed to her. That won a little gasp through the crowd and even a show of surprise from her. "My apologies," he said.

"Well," she said, a little surprised again. "I guess we'll have to learn to live with this situation for a while longer. Don't fret, Lord Summerfield. It is enough to know that they intend to come home at all. Fae can be patient and seeing them again has convinced me that they are not held here against their will. Despite all that Prince Arinith said in your favor, I still could not be certain. Don't let this cat lead you astray, Lord Summerfield. He can be quite reckless."

"Too late," I replied. "Look where I am now."

That won a laugh of delight. We left Kala to talk to her mother, but as we walked away, I glanced at Tessa, frowning --

"I will, again, talk to the others and make certain they don't want to go back with the rest of the Cat Clan. A few might. We'll deal with it and the loss of power."

I nodded, willing to leave such things in his hands.

Vane and the rest of the Dragon Clan had taken a corner near our entry, even though they had one of their own. They'd all come, even those who still preferred to stay in Fontenelle Forest rather than The Fortress. Vane looked quite excited, which might be a problem. He tended to lose control sometimes, and we didn't want him to turn into a dragon right now. His clan did a good job of keeping him in hand, though. I needn't worry about anything going wrong there.

The night pressed on. We were, I realized, pulling off the first night without any trouble. I should have felt elated, but exhaustion was taking its toll. I danced with Kala a couple times, too aware of the people watching me.

When Queen Amata stood from her throne, everyone turned her way. I didn't know what to expect, so her words took me by surprise.

"Good people of the Winter Court, I bid you good night and give blessings freely to one and all. Go now to your rest, and we shall meet again tomorrow."

Did we survive the first day? I looked at Brandis, probably a little shocked. He nodded as though he understood. A moment later, Tessa and Kala both arrived, and my group herded me towards our exit while York escorted the Queen to her entry hall, along with the guards who stayed by her.

"Back to The Fortress," Tessa urged, reminding me that the area outside the actual Winter Court might be dangerous. "And then rest while we can."

"Is it proper for me to leave?" I asked as I watched the others heading for their halls.

"Yes," Tessa said and nudged me onward. "Almost everyone will go back to the fae realm and return tomorrow. They're not going to abandon the fae lands and their clan holdings just to party for a few days. That would be an invitation to disaster."

"I suppose so. And there's so much going on back at The Fortress that we dare not stay away for long, either."

"Exactly."

I was glad enough to head down the hall toward the portal. So much yet to do --

Something attacked.

I didn't see it at first. Brandis gave a shout and shoved me aside, and I tumbled with Tessa going down as well. Then I realized that Tessa wasn't trying to get back up. Blood ran from a cut down his chest and arm, while Brandis fought off something huge and growling. My guard had called up his sword, and I wished I had one right then as well -- but then I noticed that Tessa's sword was still in his hand. I pried it from his fingers and hoped it did not disappear. I stood and swung, surprising Brandis as much as I did the enemy, but it worked for the moment we needed. By then others were rushing into the fray. That was good because the creature had turned his attention to me, and his long arm reached past both our swords to catch me in the shoulder. I didn't feel the pain yet --

The Queen's guards swarmed the creature and killed it so quickly that I hardly realized what had happened as it disappeared. Queen Amata stepped forward, frowning --

And I went down to my knees beside Tessa, who still hadn't moved. I was about to fall flat on my face, but York caught hold of me, magic easing the sudden pain of the wound.

"Tessa," I whispered, pushing York that way. "Take care of Tessa!"

York didn't argue, though he did use one more surge of magic to make certain I didn't fall over before he moved to Tessa. I saw magic sweep out from York's hands; bright and strong which meant this was a dangerous wound.

The Queen's guard spread out, protecting her, but protecting us as well. Good. I had to trust her or else there was no hope. I tried to stand, but Kala had arrived and put a hand on my shoulder, shaking her head in mute disagreement. I looked around. Brandis talked to one of the guards, his own arm bleeding as well.

"What attacked us?" I asked. My voice sounded shaky, and I dared not look at Tessa, though I was aware that York still worked with him. I could feel the magic, warm and bright.

"I don't know," Brandis answered as he glanced back at me. "But it was sent by magic. Covered by magic -- easy to do in a place with so much magic everywhere. We're trying to trace the creature, Lord Summerfield."

"Carefully," I said. "Be very careful."

He nodded agreement and glanced sideways at the Queen, as though wondering what she might still be doing here. I thought she might be remaining out of kindness since with her guards here we were both protected from any new danger and from the other fae who were crowding at the end of the hall, interested in what had happened.

"I am surprised to see the Bard of the Dragon Clan working so hard to save the Totem of the Cat Clan," Queen Amata suddenly said.

I started to speak, but it was Kala who answered before I could. "Matters are no longer the way they were in the fae lands, my Queen," she said, her voice soft. "So much changed when we learned of the lies and deceit that had kept us trapped in this realm. I want to know where Gryn is right now."

"Oh, careful, Kala," I said and finally managed to get to my feet. I felt numb, and I suspected that might be York's work. "There are plenty of others who are not happy with my new position."

Kala frowned and gave a nod of her head. Queen Amata said nothing more on the matter and I wondered what she judged in those few words.

York stood. I looked at him with worry --

"It is too dangerous to take Tessa back through the portal just now," he said. He looked shaky enough that I caught hold of his arm. "Thank you, my Lord. We need to let him rest here, for at least a day."

Here was a test I had not expected. I had always trusted Tessa more than any of the others and expected him to be at my side. I wanted him safe, so I only nodded agreement.

"Who is going to stay with him to keep Tessa safe?"

"He will have my guards," Queen Amata replied. I could see others behind the guards, and they looked surprised by the declaration. I bowed my head in thanks to her, feeling more than a little unsteady again.

"I'll also stay with Tessa," York added. He smiled at the Queen. "Best not to let the Cat Clan totem wake up and think something has happened to Summerfield."

"He has always had a reputation for being rash," Queen Amata agreed. I couldn't tell if she joked or not.

"I'll go with Lord Summerfield," Kala added. "Brandis and I will keep him safe."

Kala reached over and healed a little more of my wounds. Though she didn't have as sure a touch as York, her magic did help.

"I've set our people to the work of finding out what they can," Brandis said. He still had his sword in hand. "And yes, they will do so carefully, Lord Summerfield. You realize that no one is happy with what happened here, right? We are still within the confines of the Winter Court."

I hadn't thought about that part and grimaced. I had told Tessa that I would create a problem here. I looked down at him finally. Tessa appeared calm, though a little pale.

"With your leave?" I said and bowed to the Queen again.

She gave a nod. I walked away with the warlords of the Cat Clan and the Dragon Clan and I never doubted they would keep me safe. However, I hadn't counted on not having Tessa beside me. I felt a little chill as we left the ice palace.

CHAPTER 12

I had not expected more trouble even before we got back to The Fortress.

We were in the portal; just ten steps from one place to another. My thoughts were on Tessa and hoping he would recover quickly for his own sake. I was also thinking about how dangerous it was to be in my company --

Something was wrong.

A bright light surrounded us -- warm light and filled with a power I didn't understand. Confusing light, as though I couldn't tell which way I'd been moving a moment before.

"Damn!" Kala shouted. She grabbed hold of me with her fingers tight on my arm. "Brandis! Keep a connection to us --"

We moved, like in a maelstrom. Light swarmed around us with a power that should have torn us apart and I felt as though we danced through a tornado. I grabbed hold of Kala as well and maybe we did waltz there to the power of nature.

And then we dropped.

Sand.

Hot day.

I felt ill as I sat up and was glad to see Kala looking so alert. She got to her feet and pulled me up, but she looked worried.

"Brandis still has a tie to us," she said. "He'll get us

home."

A shadow crossed over us, and I turned -- oh yes, not in the least bit surprised to find our previously unwanted guest standing over us. I still wasn't sure whom I dealt with, but I was not at all surprised to see the tell from my dream behind him. This was his place of power, though time had reduced it to nothing more than a pile of dust and broken bricks.

Storm clouds began to gather on the horizon, a strange sight in the desert. Sand started to swirl. I lifted a shaky hand, aware that Kala still had tight hold of me. Good. I didn't want to lose her -- or see her go and find myself left behind.

"You are not one of them, and yet they follow you," the stranger said. His voice echoed wildly across the sandy desert and somewhere a dog howled.

"He is the Lord of our Clan."

I wished Kala had stayed quiet and the focus had stayed on me. The stranger frowned, and the clouds drew closer -- and that made me think I had a better idea of whom I dealt with here. He frowned, his dark eyes glaring at me.

"You are not what you appear to be either," he said finally. "You are human, but humans bow down to me. Humans *serve* me."

"The world has changed," I said. "You know this, don't you? You are from the far past, and this is not your time or place any longer."

Perhaps those were not the most sensible way to address and ancient god, but I suspected that telling him anything but the truth would have been far more dangerous. I had to get a better handle on this one, though. I needed a name because names are things of power.

"You do not know your place," he said, his voice a growl in the growing wind.

Those words were true on so many levels that I could only bow my head in agreement. Lord Summerfield of the fae didn't know his place. And I had spent such a strange life, moving so often as a child, that I never developed that feel of *home* that so many others held dear.

However, I shook that feeling away and looked back at him. He apparently didn't like the look because his eyes narrowed. The wind blew harder, and lighting struck the ground far too close to us.

And by those signs, I suddenly knew whom I dealt with in this desert place.

"Dagan, Lord of the Strom," I said aloud, partly for Kala's sake, so she knew the name. "God of the Assyrians --"

"You know who I am, and yet you do not fear me. Unwise."

He lifted his hand. Kala started to move to protect me as I yelled for her to get back. I even tried to shake her hand from my arm, but she would not let go.

"Loyal," Dagan said. "That will not save you --"

And Brandis yanked us out.

I had the feel of Brandis and his magic, so I caught hold of the thread as tightly as I could, focusing all my mind on that sense of him. Kala and I held tightly to each other as we came back in a rollercoaster of magic, sound, and movement. I felt ill and frightened that we were lost in the maelstrom and would never get out. I couldn't convince myself this was better than letting Dagan kill us --

Then we were suddenly back in the portal. Brandis was

not alone here. I recognized Lady Ethna of the Cat Clan and Vane as well as many others.

"We need to get out of here," Brandis said and caught hold of me, though Kala still had hold of the other arm. York had healed that wound and cleaned the clothing and repaired it. Good. "We are far too vulnerable."

We moved, even though I wanted to protest. Kala's mother patted her daughter on the shoulder as we passed, and I saw a look of distrust cast my way. I couldn't blame her. If I could have shaken Kala off and into her care, I would have done so.

Whatever was still affecting me was not affecting Kala the same way. I started to get annoyed and then realized it was a good thing the others were still doing so well. I wanted them to stay strong because we were in a hellish lot of trouble --

We passed into The Fortress. I pulled at the two warlords, stopping them from rushing on. I took a couple of deep breaths and even managed to get free of their hold.

"I figured out who we are up against," I said with a glance back at the portal. "He is called, among other names, Dagan. He's the ancient Assyrian god of weather."

"Weather," Brandis said and snorted. "Of course, he's associated with weather because we don't have enough trouble with the weather already."

"The trouble we have with weather might even be what made part of the connection," I pointed out. I did not have to tell these people to be careful. "What should I know about Tessa?"

"He'll be fine," Kala assured me and I knew she would not lie to Lord Summerfield. "He needs to rest so he can recover. Let's get you to your apartment. You look like hell, Summerfield."

I could hardly remain on my feet as we moved past the children's castle and on to the garage where construction of the ballroom had gone on while we were elsewhere. We passed through under a veil that hid us. The carpenters had done nice work. I appreciated it as best I could and just went on to the stairs.

They detoured me to the elevator, which I appreciated. At least it was fast, and I was soon sitting on the sofa in my apartment. I leaned back, aware that Brandis and Kala talked around me, but too tired to even listen. I could rest here.

Except Dagan could walk through the walls and the wards made by some powerful fae.

"I don't know why this has hit him so badly," Kala admitted and settled on the sofa beside me. "The journey unsettled me, but it seems to have made him ill."

"Better," I said and lifted my head. I almost meant it.

"Good." She smiled and looked at the balcony where the wind blew harder than it had when we first arrived. "He's not happy."

"We'll have to figure out how to deal with him," I said with a sigh. I stood. "I suggest we all get some rest while we can."

I limped off to my room and went to bed, though I couldn't sleep. Too many things were going on, too much input and it all followed me into sleep so that I did not rest nearly as well as I would have liked. The nightmares rolled one into another so that I fought snow in the heat of a sandy desert and held my family gathering in the ice palace.

I wanted to either sleep better or wake up --

"Maybe we need to get Tessa," Brandis said from somewhere near me. I was glad to know he was there.

"Not yet" York replied softly. His hand brushed against my arm and pains eased again. "If Tessa tried anything to help, he'd go back to a kitten. I don't think we want that right now."

"Raising two totems?" Brandis replied and sounded appalled. "No, that's not a good idea."

I must have chuckled a little. York's hand patted my arm. "Rest, Summerfield. All is fine."

So, I did sleep for a while longer, though the nightmares were no better. I finally gave up. A shower helped, and I wandered out into the other room to find York there having tea and cookies with Brandis. A glance at the window settled my mind and my plan.

"I'm going to work for a few hours," I told them. Brandis got to his feet, shaking his head. "I need a little normalcy back in my life. It's only a couple blocks away, and I can reassure people there that all is fine."

York was the one who nodded. Kala had come out of the kitchen and sat down a cup of tea for me. "Drink that first. It will give you a little extra strength. Then I'll walk you to your office. No, you cannot argue with me on this one. Tessa would skin us -- probably really skin us -- if we let you go wandering off alone now."

She was right. Tessa would probably kill me just out of exasperation. I drank my tea, and we left a little later. I felt better at the idea of doing something normal again.

Oh yeah. Working for Woo Woo News counted for normal in my life.

Kala walked with me, and we stopped just before Julia or Pam looked out the window and saw her.

"Go on in," she said. "Tessa has strong wards up on this building, too. Nothing should get in except for Dagan, of course, but we can't do anything about him either way. I'll stay out here just in case there is some trouble, though."

"You'll be cold," I protested.

"I'm fae," she replied with a bright smile. "I won't be cold, and I won't waste power. We must be safe, though, Summerfield. Protecting you is the best use of my time right now. I'd be a fool to walk away and think you'll be perfectly safe. I don't believe you want that, right?"

"No," I agreed with a laugh. I patted Kala on the arm and headed for the door. When I looked back, I couldn't see her, but I knew she stood there.

We had a festive day in the office since Julia and Pam were preparing the place for the Winter Solstice party of their own. We moved desks from the room where Tessa and I usually worked, and I helped to hang some of the decorations. Even some of the guys from the printing press downstairs came up to help.

"Tessa is handling some stuff of his own," I explained when Pam asked. They were used to him coming and going as he pleased. "I'm sure he'll be here for the gathering."

They didn't see the moment of worry before I turned away. I fussed with more of the decorations until Pam and Julia finally kicked me out of the room. I went to Julia's office with my laptop where I pretended to do some work. I rested, though. That was probably the most important part.

I'd be going back to the fae part after work. I did the

quick mental math and realized that would be around noon on their schedule. After a showing there, I could come back and attend Julia's party. I thought all of this might work as long as I didn't need sleep.

Oh yeah, Sunflower Breeze Summerfield, Lord of the fae and party guy. I did not pound my head against the wall, though it might have helped.

I did a quick check of the Internet and found reference to a freak desert storm in a remote area of Iran. I made a note of the location just in case I turned up there again. I'd point it out to the rest of the clan, too. The nearest place of safety on foot was -- well, too far to be safe, actually. I'd have to rely on magic to get me back out again.

I read over the report. If nothing else, my friends and I were keeping the meteorologists entertained this year.

I felt better. Maybe I had just needed to get away from the fae for a little while and remember that I was not, really, one of them. I had few minutes to myself, and I thought about my life. Yeah, that was scary. However, I feared I had lost track of my human side. So, I sat there and wrote some emails to my sisters, saying all was going well, but I was so busy that I likely wouldn't see them before the party. They were not to panic. I had everything in hand.

I imagined their reactions and laughed.

I glanced out the office window and was not at all surprised to see a familiar van sitting across the street. I still had no idea who they were, though after the talk with Pablo's friend, I had a good idea what trouble was about and that meant were most likely police or even government agents. The realization didn't do much for my state of mind.

I didn't need complications right now. I wished --

Oh no. I didn't wish anything at all.

"You look bothered, Summerfield," Julia said as she came into the office.

I started to get up, but she waved me back down, and she sprawled into a seat across from me. I glanced back at the computer and then to her again.

"I have to hold the party for the family this year," I said, which was just one of the *many* things bothering me, but something I could discuss with her. "I'm rebuilding part of the basement for it. Things had better go well."

"Pam told me. She said you look harassed."

"I am dealing with my sisters far more intimately than I like to do," I admitted. She tried to hide her slight smile. "It's going well, but I'm bound to panic."

"Let me know if there's anything I can do to help."

She meant those words. I smiled my thanks and we both looked up as the wind rattled the window. The weather was changing, but at least that wasn't unusual for this time of year. So far, the weather reports hadn't been filled with crazed people trying to figure out how something was happening like they had been last summer.

"It's time to go home, Summerfield," Julia said. "I'll see you at the party."

I smiled and stood, feeling better. I trusted the fae to handle all the problems on their end. Pablo and his friends were doing an admirable job of fixing things up for the family party. Even the cook had come by and been more than pleased.

So, all was well.

Pam walked back to The Fortress with me. I thought that might not be safe, but I couldn't very easily tell her to go on, and I'd walk behind her. Besides, I felt Kala following us. Maybe Pam was safer walking with me. She was so happy about the coming holidays that her joy proved to be infectious. We sang Christmas Carols. Others laughed and joined in as we passed.

Yes, I felt better. Human. Ready for anything.

CHAPTER 13

Before long, I was back in my court clothing and getting ready to make another appearance at the Winter Court. I was nervous. Hell, even Brandis was nervous, which didn't help at all.

"I am having fae go in first," Brandis explained as some of my people headed into the tunnel. "They're going to line the path. If anything tries for you again and we can't stop it, just keep tight hold of Kala. We have a strong tie to her."

"But not to me?"

"I have a tie to you, too. So do both Tessa and Kala," he said. Then he shrugged. "But Kala can reinforce the link if she needs to. That can be a big help if you get whisked away again."

That made sense. "I wish --"

Kala tackled me. We hit the ground, and I almost cursed, but she had her hand over my mouth.

Ah.

Brandis offered a hand to help me back up. "You need to stop doing that, Summerfield."

"Sorry," Kala apologized. "Tessa said to move quickly and make certain you don't finish that line."

"Yeah," I said and brushed a bit of dust from my sleeve. "Okay. Let's go."

I reminded myself to be wiser as we stepped into the tunnel. The place was still beautiful, but I held my breath, and we hurried the ten steps and slipped out into the ice palace. The hall there wasn't much safer, of course. Brandis stood at my back and York had been waiting and took the opposite side from Kala. We came out into the main room filled with fae and music. Did I think I was safer here rather than in the tunnel? I happened to spot Roan who was hard to miss. He stayed in Centaur form, even here where all the other clan totems were in fae form instead. Gryn stood not far away from Roan, and I saw the smirk Gryn gave me. Kala's hand tightened on my arm, and I knew she saw him too.

We would not break the truce.

I turned away and walked with my friends to greet the Queen who sat on the throne. I gave her a proper bow and she nodded in return. Her eyes narrowed, but she was looking past me, so I didn't think my presence had annoyed her. I didn't look behind me, though I hated the feel of danger at our backs.

"I am not happy with what happened, Lord Summerfield," Queen Amata said. She looked at me and then gave a slight bow of her head with a softening of her stare. "However, I do not blame you."

I decided it was wise to be honest. Being less so with any fae was never wise, and even more so with the Queen.

"This might be my fault," I admitted. Queen Amata looked at me, blinking in surprise and confusion. "This trouble might be because of who I am. Unfortunately, there is nothing I can do to change that part."

She nodded. "The Winter Court is always held with an

understanding of truce. It should not matter who or what you are. You are here in a place where we have set aside old problems. I am still not happy with the others, Lord Summerfield. There will be a reckoning for what they've done."

I knew better than to argue with the Queen. Kala's hand had tightened on my arm again, and I think she believed I would do something unwise. Instead, I bowed and stepped away into the crowd.

I mingled with Kala always at my side. She no doubt looked fierce enough that she kept the others polite when they dealt with me. We had a bigger crowd today. I had the feeling that the trouble drew some others in to see what would happen. I was the entertainment, I supposed.

We met some more of the Cat Clan people. Kala was happy to talk with them, and I thought she should have been with them rather than babysitting me.

She must have seen the look in my eyes. Kala patted my arm, which surprised the others.

"I am where I need to be, Summerfield. Yes, even as the Cat Clan Warlord, this is still where I should be. I am with you because you are the center of the battle. You brought us together with Dragon Clan and ended a war that might have gone on for centuries more if Gryn had had his way."

"True," Lady Ethna said with a glance around the room. "Miserable little coward. Kala is wise. She knows what she needs to do."

"I don't mean to keep her away from your clan."

"I know. We discussed the matter."

Kala smiled. "We are living in a whole new world. Even

though I had been in your realm for a long time, I never really *lived* there. Not like Tessa has done. It isn't often fae get the chance to do something new."

"I hadn't thought about it that way." I recalled some of what the others had taught me about the clans, rules, and ancient wars that had gone on for far too long. I brought something new into the system. Maybe that wasn't all bad.

I started paying more attention to the people around me in this unique celebration. They were enthralled by everything human, and it seemed as though the magical aspects of the place were excellent, but the food was exquisite. Even the cloth of my clan drew some attention, along with the colors.

Were they a people trapped in one way of life for a long, long time? Not stagnant in some ways, but in others, they were unable to see ahead enough to make changes. They could use magic to get what they needed for survival, and the future was always there so they need not worry about doing anything too quickly.

There was much I didn't like about my world, but at least we kept moving ahead. Interesting way to look at things. I realized being human, and having that outside view, was power in a way I had not expected.

I had been thinking about this when I realized someone had moved to get between Kala and me. I turned to step back to join her and saw another move closer --

Several people with blurred faces stood around me. Most of them wore gray -- Wolf Clan colors -- but I realized that could be a deception since they hid their faces. Someone grabbed my arm, and before I could shout a protest, a hand went over my mouth.

They couldn't possibly think they would get me out of here in the midst of this crowd! Not all the fae could be in on this --

I kicked. Someone grunted. Another person jabbed a fist into my stomach, and I doubled over -- and realized that they were not using magic, which would make it harder for my friends to track me.

The music grew louder, but only because we had moved closer to the orchestra which meant -- no big surprise -- that we were heading towards the Centaur Hall.

I didn't want to go through that hall. I fought one arm free and used it to shove someone away. They hadn't expected my strength, I think. They were too used to working with magic.

I thought I could hear Kala shout above the music. Then I caught a glimpse of Gryn smiling my way. No, that couldn't be good.

I kept trying to fight and expecting someone to use magic to stop me, but that would have drawn attention. I shoved again and thought I could hear Brandis now as well. They were coming closer, which must have meant that he knew where they were going.

Gryn came closer, though. Something sharp jabbed into my arm. "That will keep him quiet."

Oh yes. Gryn had been in my realm long enough to know about drugs. Damn. I felt whatever he had given me starting to pull me down into some dark, empty place I did not want to go. We were to the hall. I could not get away. Kala and Brandis shouted, but I couldn't make out their words. Everything slipping away.

They even took the hand from my mouth since I could hardly move now. Damn. No hope --

And then Tessa arrived.

I had not expected him. He looked pale and thin, but the fire in his eyes made me realize what was going to happen before the others did.

He turned cat. Between one breath to the next, he leapt in amongst those who had hold of me. The people screamed and dropped me to the ground. They scattered, but unfortunately, some of them were scattering right over the top of me, and I couldn't do anything to protect myself. It hurt, but in a distant, drug-fogged way.

Kala caught hold of me. Good. I even felt a tendril of magic working through me. People shouted everywhere, but Tessa was already back to his fae form and had a cleared circle of everyone around us.

I ached, and my head started to pound with each new sound. Tessa shouted, and I couldn't even make out the words, but I could see unhappy people everywhere and not a few worried looks in my direction. I wasn't certain if they were worried about me or about what was going to happen now. I couldn't decide anything with my head pounding.

"Please," I whispered when Kala started to shout as well. No one sounded happy. "Please, please be quiet."

And they fell silent, everyone -- but I knew that didn't come from my request.

Queen Amata stepped into the opening, her face set in anger. Everyone took a step backward, and Kala put a hand on my arm as though to hold me still -- even though I couldn't move. In fact, I was having more trouble breathing.

York arrived, looked at Tessa with a shake of his head, and dropped down beside me. He took over from Kala, and I could feel his stronger magic moving in through my body. The next breath finally came a little easier, and I was starting to hear more clearly. It felt as though a heavy blanket was being pulled away, inch by inch.

The Queen was not happy, which meant there could be the sort of breach here that I so desperately didn't want to happen. I thought if I could get up, we might get everything in order. Get back to the party.

I did not want to see a war started over this.

The silence helped me get some of my controls back. I tried to sit up, but York held me down with a silent shake of his head. I could hear whispers now, and I wasn't certain if Queen Amata spoke or not. Probably something I didn't want to hear anyway.

"I need --" I said, but even my voice sounded too loud now.

Tessa came over and all but threw himself onto the floor beside me. He still looked angry, but when he reached out to help me, it was York who knocked his hand away.

"Don't be a fool. That would just put you down again," York said. "We need you stronger."

The Queen looked at us, shocked. I didn't know why until I realized that the *Dragon Clan Bard* had slapped aside the *Cat Clan Totem*. She had not quite gotten used to that change yet.

Tessa was not upset, though. He looked at me and gave a little shake of his head. "Things are not going as well as we hoped."

I laughed and tried to find Gryn again, but he was

nowhere in sight, of course. I knew he wouldn't be.

Many people looked at us with shock and dismay. I knew that came from the fear that I was going to do something that demanded they take action. I would have loved to point them right at Gryn right now --

But I still didn't want to start that war. We had survived -- I looked around quickly until I spotted Kala and Brandis. I didn't see any of the enemies on the ground, so I assumed Tessa had not used his claws. I thought we were both being rather good about this attack.

"What brought you down here?" I asked.

"I could feel your worry, and then I caught the panic from Kala and Brandis. I still have the best connection to you so I got here as fast as I could."

"Thank you." I looked up at Queen Amata and gave a quick bow of my head. "My apologies to you and the rest of the clans. I am not looking for this sort of dramatics. Shall we get back to the celebration?"

I tried to stand, but York gave me a shake of the head. I wasn't going to be able to get up without his help, so I didn't argue.

Kala finally reached over and put a hand on my arm. "I am sorry, Lord Summerfield, that I lost you. I'm appalled that this happened --"

"They worked extremely hard to do this right, Kala. I don't blame you," I said. "We all knew something was bound to happen.

"I could not get close enough to see who took you," she said. She looked at Tessa. Did you?"

"They wore mask spells," he said with a snarl and then

looked at me. "Those are spells that are so small they'd go unnoticed in a place filled with this much magic."

"But we know where they headed," York said with a nod to the hall not far from us.

"That could have been a ploy to make everyone look to the Centaur Clan," I replied before the others spoke. They all gave reluctant nods.

"The Centaur Clan Totem was with me when this happened," Queen Amata admitted.

Of course he was, I thought. Roan would never be in any place where he might be in danger, though he might work to keep the Queen busy and not looking for the human. Tessa did the one thing I didn't want, though. He looked straight at me and asked a question I wished he hadn't. "Did you see who it was?"

"Do you think we can get up off the floor now?" I asked with a shake of my head. "This is rather undignified, you know."

Tessa gave me an odd look; he knew I had evaded the question, but this was not the time to say that I had seen Gryn and that he'd been the one with the needle. I rubbed at my arm where he'd jabbed me and thought I might like to do the same to him at another time. In fact, I looked forward to it.

I didn't want more trouble at the Winter Court. I wanted these days to go calmly, and if that meant I had to chain myself to Kala, that's what I'd do. We were going to get through this with me alive and no war.

I got back to my feet, though it did take Kala to keep me there. York helped Tessa to his feet, and he didn't look any better than I did.

"Maybe you had better go back and rest, Tessa," I suggested.

"That's not going to happen," he replied and pulled free from York. "I could go back to the room, but I would not rest. I'll do better staying with you, Summerfield."

So, we got everyone moving. The music started up again. Queen Amata went back to her throne where others had gathered. I couldn't see Roan around, but he'd be quick to leave if he thought he might find himself implicated.

I had Tessa to my right, Kala to my left and Brandis behind me. I feared I was going to get knocked down and trampled by my people at this point. I finally got York to go off and deal with the party while the four of us went off to a somewhat quiet corner. No one was in a hurry to come too close, and I figured that had to do with the snarls on all our faces.

"Okay, what did you see? Who did you see?" Tessa finally asked.

Brandis was just moving beside Tessa since I now had my back to the wall. He looked startled. So did Kala.

"Gryn, of course," I mumbled. I saw them all turn, eyes scanning the floor. "He won't have stayed any longer than Roan remained when the trouble started. We can't do anything about it just now."

"You should have said," Kala replied.

"No. We don't want a battle here, Kala. Even if I said, there would be some who wouldn't believe me."

Brandis agreed though he still looked around with eyes narrowed as though he could read the guilt in the faces of those around him. This situation was going to get worse unless

I could find a way to divert my people's attention again. That didn't look likely, especially since I was not happy either. Controlling my anger was not going to be easy. And it was, really, a good thing Gryn was not anywhere in sight.

"At least we got to you in time," Kala said. She had tight hold of my arm again. I was going to have bruises on top of bruises. "I don't know what would have happened if they had gotten you out of here."

"Oh, I think we all know what would have happened," Brandis replied, which did not set well with the others.

I lifted a hand, willing it to be still. People started to move, then seemed to remember that I had no magic (at least as far as they knew).

"We need to return to the festivities," I said to the few strangers who had dared to come close. "If we let this continue, it only lets *them* win this round. My friends have done an extraordinary job to create this Winter Court. Please take the time to enjoy it."

The others gave nods, some of them even gracious and polite, obviously glad to have things return to normal. Brandis took the spot behind me again, and Tessa stayed at my side. We moved into the crowd, and I tried not to wince every time I thought someone was coming too close. We paused at the food -- the last thing I wanted right now -- and then on towards the side of the room with the exit to my hall. Good. We could get out quickly if we had to. I was ready to bolt, but I stayed polite to everyone who stopped to talk, and it seemed they relaxed more for it, even if neither my people nor I did as well.

"The Queen has not yet confirmed you as Lord

Summerfield," Tessa suddenly said. "We're still in limbo."

"She's done that before," Brandis added. "Don't worry yet. She also hasn't limited our powers. However, if she declines your claim, we're going to be scrambling to get you to safety. She could make the announcement at any of these gatherings now, so be ready."

The other two nodded and looked worried again.

I felt a bit of a chill again. "I don't want you to put yourselves in danger," I whispered. "I don't want --"

Tessa shook his head, and I knew enough to fall silent.

"If we abandoned you now, my fine Lord Summerfield, we would not be counted for much among the fae, no matter what the outcome of the Queen's decision."

"So, we will still do our best to make certain you are safe," Kala added. She gave a bright smile. "We'd do that for a friend, you know."

Okay, I couldn't argue with any of those points. I should have considered this from the full view of fae honor, which I was starting to understand very well.

The music had started up again. People began to laugh and dance, the worries of the attack slipping away as I made as little of it as I could. My head still buzzed, and I felt unsteady, but we put on a good show.

"Tessa, Kala -- I'm correct that you and the Cat Clan people could get home now that you have contact with people from the rest of the clan who are in the fae lands, right?"

Tessa gave me a look of tried patience which amused everyone else. Even Kala, who had looked far too grim, gave a sudden laugh. I thought Tessa might have done it on purpose, but even so, he knew I wasn't going to walk away from the question. Tessa leaned back against the wall beside me. I didn't think either of us should be on our feet right now.

"We have discussed the matter, Summerfield," he said. "We are not ready to return."

"You might not get another chance like this, Tessa. You can't think staying with me is more important after all the years you were in exile!"

Someone looked our way and I noted the gray of Wolf Clan. He appeared curious, too and I had the feeling a lot of people wondered about the actions of the Cat Clan exiles.

Tessa reached over and put a hand on my arm, which drew quite a few more stares. I wondered what was wrong. Was it that I was human? That he was the Cat Clan Totem? That I was (or might not be, depending on the whim of the Queen), a fae lord?

This situation was getting to be far too complicated.

I felt as though there was still far too much I didn't understand and too much I feared to ask. I didn't want to step over any lines. Tessa, though, could read my moods.

"Things have been odd in your reality, Summerfield," he said.

"Oh? I hadn't noticed."

He had started to say something but stopped this time and grinned. People laughed and not all of them my people. That helped again, I thought. Good.

But he had also triggered something in my thoughts, and I gave a quick nod finally.

"Things are odd," I agreed and worked my way through the thought. "Things are occurring there that shouldn't be happening. That's why you're staying."

"Part of it," Tessa agreed. And yes, we were drawing more people to listen in. I thought it might not hurt to have others know what was going on.

"The trouble is a good part of why we remained," Tessa said. "Dragon Clan could have gotten us back before this, you know. However, you have made it possible for all of us to work there in ways we couldn't have otherwise. If we didn't have that ability, who would stop the others? Who would have stopped the Dvergar? Who would have stopped the trolls?"

I noticed some odd looks from others as we talked. I thought they might not have considered the full extent of the problem of this happening in a place where there was no local access to magic. Someone even asked Brandis a few questions, and we rested there and listened to excellent music. York played a couple of times. I could tell he was a favorite with the entire group. Vane came and stood by me, worried and silent, but I reassured him all was well, and he went back to enjoy himself. The last thing we needed was for the young Dragon Clan Totem to lose control and shift.

Like Tessa had. No one seemed to be making much out of that part of the incident, and I had to wonder how often the somewhat wild totems gave such a show at one of the courts.

Others danced. I saw Gryn and Roan had returned and were across the room, but they didn't dare come near me. We'd get through this gathering without any more trouble.

And then all I had to do was worry over Dagan tonight.

Rest. At least I could rest for a while longer.

"Time to go, Lord Summerfield," Kala said, tapping my arm.

I pushed away from the wall and braced my legs before I

gave a nod of agreement. I hadn't noticed the group thinning out, but Queen Amata had stood as well, and gave the nod in my direction. I bowed my head and only kept from falling flat on my face but Tessa's sudden grab.

"Sorry," I apologized, but Tessa waved it off and let Kala take hold of me.

We headed for the tunnel, which set my adrenaline rushing again. I hoped the others had a plan for what they'd do if Dagan tried to take me again. We found people in the tunnel. More than my people, in fact, and I recognized a couple of the Wolf Clan, including Faris, their leader whom I had met earlier. Tessa smiled brightly and slapped Desina, the Wolf Clan Totem, on the arm. She grinned back at him.

The Queen had sent some of her guards as well. I mumbled thank you to everyone as my people rushed me towards the end of the tunnel.

Along with Tessa.

"You should stay -- rest --" I said, worried as we crossed the ten steps.

"No, this is where I need to be." We were already heading out the other end, and I looked back to see the others exiting the other way and moving in haste, wise people. "I would just fret and worry too much now. Besides, we have Julia's party, and I don't want to upset her."

"Tessa --"

Tessa put a hand on my shoulder as we paused, already in the garage. "It's part of the balance," he said. "We have too much out of balance already. I need to do what I can to help bring everything back in line to where it should be."

I could almost feel what he was saying as we headed for

the stairs.

"Elevator," Tessa said. "This is an elevator day, unless the rest of you want to carry Summerfield and me up."

The others laughed. I could look out from the little bubble of protection around us and saw the workers putting up the lighting in the remade garage.

"We are going to need a garage. We're keeping this," I said. "I had already considered the building behind us. Then an enclosed walkway between the buildings? Is that going to be a problem?"

"We should be able to include it in The Fortresses defenses," Brandis said. "Sounds like a good idea."

Nice to consider such minor things that were not going to change the world. Once they were past the holiday season, I'd start looking into the business.

We were not safer here, of course. However, I could feel The Fortress around me, the safety of a place that was mine and filled with my people.

My life had gotten far too strange, and all things considered, I never thought I would be saying something like that, given my childhood and my recent association with the fae.

We were in the hall and heading for the elevator when we saw Pablo.

"Summerfield, good," he said. "I come to say be careful. Someone still saying bad thinks about you. Stay safe."

I gave a nod of thanks.

More enemies. I didn't need more enemies. As we went into the apartment, I started listing out all the enemies I thought my give me trouble over the next few days.

I gave it up and went to rest instead.

CHAPTER 14

The one *really* good thing about Julia's parties, aside from the company, is the food. I caught the scent mingled scent of spices, sugar, chocolates -- a person could gain weight just standing in the doorway. I might find some of my lost energy here, I hoped.

The window shined with holiday lights and the welcome sign up. Cars had been parked all along the street and in our little lot to the side of the building. Tessa and I had walked up from The Fortress, huddled against the cold, with Kala and a couple of others keeping watch over us, though unseen. I could get paranoid about that kind of thing if I let myself think about it.

Laughter came from the room where the two of us usually worked, and we hung up our coats and headed there. The room felt warmer than usual. Friendly.

We joined in the festivities. Looking around, I had an odd feeling about the fae and how structured everything felt in the Winter Court. That might be necessary with so many powerful people because a few of them might not be happy to see each other.

I worried about their reactions to me, but I was not going to carry that attitude over to this gathering. Julia and Pam had done an exceptional job of setting up this party. People were happy. I wasn't going to bring my black mood here.

I kept an eye on those who came in, though. Seemed wise, under the circumstances. Many people who made deliveries to Woo Woo news dropped in for a few minutes. So did some of our local subscribers, and while this was not a gathering with children, there was nothing crude, rude or risqué about the adult behavior.

I remembered Jacobs coming to the party drunk last year, quiet Pam following him in and looking embarrassed. She hardly seemed like the same person this year; and if Jacobs had walked in, I would have personally kicked him out on his ass.

The thought cheered me immensely.

Tessa and I mingled. He was never far from my side, but that wasn't unusual. I could introduce him to people since he had only lately joined the team. Pam was close to Julia for much the same reason.

The food was good. The people were fun.

"You two both look like you're coming down with something," Julia said when we happened to meet by the cookie tray. "Good thing that we're closed for the next week. You both need rest."

I nodded with my mouth clamped shut against what would have been hysterical laughter as I considered the next few days. More fae stuff, which wouldn't be too bad, but I would have to deal with my sisters, too. I couldn't keep skirting their calls or else they were going to come and hunt me down.

And I still hadn't come up with presents for them, either.

"I am going to need some sleep soon," I told Tessa. "This is starting to get the better of me."

"Yeah," he said. "Me too. But I'm glad we're here. It's good to remember that these are the people we are trying to protect. You aren't Lord Summerfield because you want the power."

I looked around and nodded, feeling better again. Maybe I was losing touch with humanity. I'd have to think about how to correct this possible problem.

"I hope no one else tries anything at the Winter Court," he continued. I was surprised he brought it up here -- but maybe that was because we were outside the fae realm and he could talk without too much worry. "I think even Gryn and Roan are smart enough not to annoy Queen Amata any more than they have. They pushed Wolf Clan closer to our side, and that was no easy trick. I'm sure Roan, at least, is worried. That's not a clan to upset."

"I don't doubt it. Who is the leader of the Dragon Clan?"

"They haven't chosen one yet. Brandis would likely take the role, but right now they're still in flux. They need a warlord more than they need a clan leader. They might be waiting for Vane to help make the choice."

That made sense in a fae sort of way. They had no reason to hurry anything.

"I'm going to have to look better by the time we have the family party," I said. "I don't dare look like I'm half dead or they'll ask questions, and I don't want to consider lying to them."

"Not a good idea, you're right. We have things under control, or else others wouldn't let the two of us out even for this little gathering. And that's Lenz at the door."

I looked for the local police officer who had fallen in with us and knew far too much about the fae and me. I missed him the first time; he was not in uniform, and he'd kept his coat and hat on, even coming into the group. He wasn't the only one, so he didn't look too odd, just one of the many who only stopped by for a moment.

"He doesn't want the others to notice him," Tessa said. "Move back to the corner by the punch. I can keep the three of us hidden there for a short while."

"Tessa --"

"He's here for a reason. We'll make this fast."

I had learned not to argue with Tessa when he had that look on his face. Lenz had something to tell us, and Tessa seemed to think it might be important. So much for calm and fun.

Lenz spotted us and came our way, though not a straight line that would have drawn attention. That gave me a little time to calm again. And eat another cookie. I needed the energy, right?

His arrival meant some new trouble, but I couldn't get up enough energy to worry. We'd take care of the problem, whatever it was. I had to believe that my people and I could handle whatever came our way, but I was starting to worry about Karma again and what I'd done wrong to get all of this dumped on me at the same time.

When he finally reached us, Tessa gave a little flicker of his fingers and a fine line of magic drew up around us, dulling out the sounds of the rest of the party.

"I am *never* going to get used to that, you know," Lenz said with a slight frown at Tessa. "A good plan, though. I came to let you know that I started hearing bad things on the street,

Summerfield."

I should have realized. I gave Lenz a quick nod. "I heard the same from Pablo and some of his friends. I've heard that there are rumors out there that I am a drug lord. Not good."

"Things have gone beyond the drug lord level," Lenz said, which sent a chill through me again. "We've heard rumors at the force that you are leading a cult in your building and that you have an army hidden away in there. You're getting shipments of what could be guns at very odd hours."

"Supplies," I said, startled and gave a wave of my arms. "Building things. A castle for the children and a room to hold my family gathering this year."

"People are saying you are settling in for a siege."

"Well, damn," I said, startled by this news despite myself.

Lenz gave a quick nod and glanced back at the others. Tessa looked bothered, too.

"This is starting to look more dangerous than I expected," I said, but I couldn't say that surprised me, given the way things had been going lately. A cult? Weapons? No, I didn't want anyone to think that was something we had going on. We had to get this fixed.

"Someone is doing a job on you, Summerfield," Lenz said. "I don't know who, but there are rumors that some people are taking this seriously. I've stayed clear of it so far --"

"Keep doing so," I said hastily. "Don't get dragged in trying to defend us. There's no reason for it."

Lenz gave a reluctant nod of agreement, but I couldn't tell if he was going to listen to me or not.

"This isn't anything you can fight," Tessa said. "You say the wrong thing and others will assume you are in with us."

"It might be --"

"We can pull out of this," Tessa said. "We'll likely do it without magic, too. We are none of the things they claim."

"I know," he said. "And I would like to say that good always wins out, but you have to be careful. If word got out of the real stuff that's going on --"

"It would change your world," Tessa said and got a startled look from Lenz. "But remember that we have been here for a long time. We're careful."

"You need to find out who is making the claims."

"I'll look into it," I said. The shock was giving way to anger. "This could be someone with a grudge against the Summerfield family. It's happened before. I am an easy target for that kind of harassment because I choose to live outside the family."

They both nodded, neither of them looking happy. We didn't need more trouble.

"Thank you for the news," I said. "But try to stay clear of it, Lenz. Really."

He nodded reluctant agreement. Lenz did not like to see anyone blamed for things they hadn't done and that made him careful of his work.

Tessa lowered the shield and Lenz grabbed something to drink and moved away. He didn't leave the party right away. Wise man. I realized that I should have mentioned that I was being watched, but it seemed likely, under the circumstances that he had already figured that part out.

"I am starting to think I shouldn't be out like this," I said. "I am putting others in danger too --"

"No," Tessa said. He even put a hand on my arm. "You

have to go on as though everything is normal. Otherwise, people will start seeing guilt where there is only caution and worry."

"I don't want to draw others into danger with me, Tessa. This trouble is getting way out of hand."

"We'll get it worked out." I realized I had started to draw some attention, forgetting that he'd dropped the shield. Not enough sleep and too much going on. "You have extraordinary protection, Summerfield, at least as things go in this world. We won't let anything happen to you if we can stop it. If you hide, though, you look as though you have something to hide."

I knew he was right. I didn't like the feel of this, though.

"Tessa, I get the feeling everything is linking together now, whether they started out that way or not. I wish -- *no*." I stopped myself just before Tessa moved to tackle me. "Sorry."

Tessa gave a slightly nervous laugh. "We're all on edge. Have another cookie."

"I'll waddle out of here."

"Yes, but you'll be happy as you waddle. These are very good."

Tessa gave me a cookie.

"Once my sisters find out about this last bit with the drug lords, Tessa, there is going to be hell to pay."

"Oh, gods," Tessa whispered. Yeah, not something he had thought about until now. I almost felt sorry for springing that part on him.

I still didn't have presents for my sisters, either.

"We need to find out who is behind this," I said at last. "I was going to leave it until after the other matters, but now I think it's going to spring before we're ready."

I looked towards the door and thought about heading home -- but no. I couldn't leave right after Lenz. The last thing we needed was for me to draw attention to him, right?

So, I might as well stay and enjoy the party. I talked with some of the others, and we joked about the wolf story and the abominable snowman sightings. I was worried about those things since the vampire sightings last October had turned out to be somewhat real. Now, though, we laughed. I ate far more sweets than I should.

Everything seemed oddly normal here, as much as anything could be for Woo Woo news. Tessa was right; we had calm here for a while and though I knew it wouldn't last, I accepted being part of the human world again.

Around midnight the weather started turning bad. Many of us stayed with Julia to celebrate that special hour, and then as the others left, Tessa, Pam and I helped to clean up.

"You need to get some rest, Summerfield," Julia said as the three of us finally headed for the door. "You and Tessa both look like you haven't slept much lately."

"Not much," I agreed. "Soon."

"The Lady's Blessings on your three," she said, which she had not said to many of others. "Go in peace, my friends. Good luck."

As though she knew something was wrong. Before I could say anything more, she had closed the door behind us.

So, we sang Christmas Carols as we headed home, and I tried to ignore that a car followed us a few blocks behind.

CHAPTER 15

I slept. No dreams, no troubles. I had the feeling Julia's Lady had looked kindly on us for a few hours.

I got up and showered, ate bagels and tea, and then dressed for the next Fae gathering. Some of my fae, looking frayed and worried, had been wandering in all morning. There had been a couple of incidents, both so obviously contrived by Gryn that he was becoming unpopular with everyone and not just my beleaguered clan.

"Much more of this and the Queen is going to send him packing," Brandis said. He looked quite pleasantly smug, and I laughed as we gathered our group and prepared for another show in the fae court.

"Any word on anything here?" I asked as we went downstairs. "Drug Lords? Ancient Assyrian Gods?"

Tessa gave a little laugh of his own this time. "Nothing to report on either side. The people in the van are still there. They've left it parked in the snow, but they trade out people. Must be damned cold and uncomfortable in there. I can't imagine why they bother."

"And no sign of Dagan," Kala added.

I counted that as good. I had feared Dagan was going to show up at Julia's party.

Then I had a worse thought and almost tripped.

"We have to figure out the Dagan problem. We can't have him show up at the Family Gathering."

Once we made it through the Winter Court, *if* I was still Lord Summerfield, there were bound to be more hurdles to face.

"Ready?" Tessa asked.

"Not really," I admitted. "But that isn't going to stop me from going through."

So we went through the portal and the hall beyond, and I barely had my breath back before we were out in the party amid loud voices and louder music.

Vane joined us and lounged against the wall looking far too much like a dandified version of James Dean. *Dragon without a Cause.* This might be bad.

"How are you doing, Vane?" I asked.

He grinned. "Nice party. But you really need to bring in pizza, you know."

We all laughed. Vane seemed far more assured, and I wondered if that came from spending more time in a place of magic rather than back in the Fontenelle Forest.

"I'll have pizza brought in," I promised. Why not? Even Tessa nodded.

I had made Vane happy. I realized that he wanted to share something he loved with the others here. Interesting. He could eat pizza any time he wanted back in Omaha.

He wandered off. I talked to some others; everything seemed far calmer today. I thought people might be accepting me. I didn't see Gryn or Roan around, either, which was probably a good thing. I kept an eye out for them (like my guards wouldn't notice the two) and did my best to enjoy the discussions. People here wanted to know about technology. That's not as easy to explain as it sounds but we were deep into the discussion when someone approached us.

"The Queen requests your presence," one of her guards said with a nod in my direction. He turned and walked away again.

Tessa looked worried, but then he had for days now.

"This could be a problem," Tessa admitted. He straightened his tunic just as I did the same. "But we have to face it sooner or later."

I couldn't tell, looking at her, what Queen Amata thought about me. She was speaking to others, and I recognized the Eagle and Wolf warlords. I couldn't tell if they were unhappy or not, either. They did look grim, but none of them turned my way.

I took a deep breath and started to join them with Tessa and Brandis at my side. I almost waved them both off, but it would be useless, and they would argue with me. Not very dignified. So, we made our way through the crowd and to the throne. People were dancing again. I'd have to do that with Kala again because I had the feeling, despite the hard as nails impression she gave, she had enjoyed waltzing.

Well, we were going to have a ballroom in the former garage. I guess we could hold dances now and then. York might enjoy having a place to play.

A club? A diner?

Not the time to think about it.

"Remember, you have protection, no matter what happens here," Tessa whispered. Brandis nodded as well, but we didn't slow.

I wished they didn't feel the need to have the two between their own people and me. I didn't want that kind of trouble. I also didn't want them to be in trouble with their Queen. If she decided to deny my right as Lord Summerfield -- and really, I couldn't see any reason why she wouldn't -- then I didn't want the rest of these people to feel obliged to stand up for me and make things worse for themselves. I still hadn't gotten through that code of theirs. What happened here would be about their honor.

She nodded in my direction as I neared, and I gave her a very proper bow.

I saw Arinith coming to join us as well. Both the warlords gave me nods, and neither looked upset. I started to relax a little, though maybe they weren't upset because I was about to be removed as Lord of the fae --

A person just can't double guess this kind of stuff. I gave it up. I'd have to trust the fae with my life. I couldn't say I always trusted their sanity, and I didn't think it had to do with the differences between humans and fae, either.

I dared a glance at Tessa to try and judge the situation.

And somewhere over his right shoulder, I spotted one of the others bringing up a gun.

My body moved faster than my conscious thoughts could catch up. I shoved Tessa aside, and he went down with a grunt of surprise. I couldn't quite make out the face of the gunman. The gun was still aiming our way, though.

"Gun!" I shouted and moved to put myself between the gunman and the Queen.

And that almost got me in more trouble as the gun aimed my way and the Queen's guards reacted to my sudden move.

The gun fired and I saw the Queen's hand move slightly before ice shatter off the throne. Part of the wall crack. A bullet hit one of the guards as well, but by then Tessa and Brandis were both aware of the trouble.

My two guards got between the gunman and us and threw magic straight at him. I saw the fae fall, but he also went down so fast that I couldn't make out the features. Tessa looked likely to go down on his knees, and I took hold of his arm. He gasped a few times and gave a weary nod.

At least this had gotten over quickly, and I thought everyone would calm down --

Someone came closer and realized I couldn't make out his face. He had something silver in his hands.

"Protect the Queen!" I shouted and then did something probably stupid, all things considered. I threw myself straight at the attacker. Took him by surprise, too.

I could hear Tessa and Brandis both shout and then curse in ways I was fairly sure they shouldn't be doing in the presence of the fae queen.

I collided with the enemy. The fae went down under me, but I had grabbed the arm with the gun and hoped everyone had the wisdom to clear away. The weapon fired twice -- almost deafening this close --

While I fought to get that gun away, he twisted, grabbed something at his waist and stabbed at me.

I had just managed to pull aside enough so that the blade cut along my arm and not into my chest. That was going to hurt like hell, but now the new attack angered me. I don't often get angry. I slugged the guy. Yeah, that hurt too, but at least I got a little satisfaction from it.

Besides, the others were not coming to my rescue quite as fast as I expected, which meant something more going on and I didn't dare stop to try and find out what it might be.

I knew the guy I was fighting was going to turn to magic at any moment and that would be the end of my battle. I had counted on the others getting here before then, though.

Tessa and Brandis were going to be very mad.

Then I heard the unmistakable roar of an enraged Tessa in cat form, followed by a different sort of roar. People rushed away, and I realized Vane had changed to dragon form as well. I'm sure it was a sight to see, but I didn't have the strength to turn.

Tessa leapt over the top of us and into the mass of people on the other side. I didn't know what he was after, but it seemed as though something changed at that moment. I couldn't see Vane, and I hoped someone had him in hand.

I hoped someone got around to helping me soon. I hoped --

Going lightheaded from the pain and the blood loss ... besides, I hadn't recovered from the last battle. My attacker finally got the better of me, and we rolled until he had pinned me under him. I wasn't going to be able to hold back the gun or the knife --

The Queen's guard grabbed him. I barely had time catch my breath before Brandis arrived, getting me on my feet.

I did see Vane, finally. He stood before the Queen with his wings spread out to protect her. People had backed away. They were still backing away. I didn't even want to go closer, and I trusted Vane.

"Damn, Summerfield," Brandis mumbled.

"I want answers," I said, though the words slurred. "I want --"

York arrived and went straight to healing the arm wound. I looked down at the person I had been fighting --

Dead. I could tell he was dead, and I shook my head, stunned.

"Brandis?" I asked. He looked at me, frowning. "I didn't kill him. I never had that much of an advantage. What the hell --"

"The other one is dead, too," Tessa said. "And a couple more in the crowd who were working with them, helping to reinforce their spells. A web of some sort tied them together, and they died together as a result. Are you okay?"

"I am growing very, very annoyed," I admitted. I gave York a nod of thanks and finally had a chance to look around. Some people had left, but the others were starting to get louder again.

"Be still and be silent!" the Queen shouted.

Oh yeah. We all went still. I didn't breathe for a moment until I feared I was going to fall over from lack of oxygen. Then I took a little gasp and another.

Vane had folded his wings and glared at everyone. I hadn't seen him in dragon form lately, and he was far larger than he used to be. If Queen Amata hadn't ordered us all to be still, I would have urged Brandis over to him. He needed calm.

The Queen came away from the throne and down the steps. She looked our way, and her eyes narrowed in anger, but I knew it wasn't directed at us this time.

"Who are those who attacked?" she asked.

"We don't know," Brandis replied softly. "They're dead,

and we didn't do it. Spellbound and their very essence wiped clear. If they were trying for Summerfield again, they were not too concerned about anyone else who might get in the way."

No one liked that implication since any of them might have been with us at the time.

Vane changed back to human form, though he looked bothered and restless.

"Get Vane calmer," I said softly to Brandis, and he gave a nod of agreement.

"We will have answers for this action," the Queen of the Fae said, but this time gave a wave of her hand. "And we will not let them control this gathering by instilling fear and worry. The trouble is no small matter, Summerfield, this break in the truce."

"My apologies," I said with a bow of my head. "My presence has surely been the root of this problem, even though this has never been my intention."

"This isn't the first time we've had a break in a solstice truce, Summerfield," she said in reply. She'd calmed which helped the others. I nudged Brandis off towards Vane, but only because Tessa had put a hand on my shoulder. "We have had rogues in the past."

"How do we know this man and his clan aren't behind all of this?" Lord Koris of the Eagle Clan asked. "What they do already is suspect. And the use of a gun -- that points to the human does it not?"

Oddly, even as he said the words, I had the feeling he didn't believe any of them. Had he put the idea out into the open so the others would discuss it rather than letting the idea run through the rumor mill? I had the odd feeling the Eagle

Clan wasn't very worried about me as a clan leader.

Queen Amata glanced my way and shook her head. "I think this might be someone trying too hard to point at Summerfield. I think someone might be using this unusual situation for his personal gain."

I said nothing, though I thought she made a good point. I saw Tessa give a little nod and his hand tightened on my arm again. We were not out of danger, nor out of being framed for this mess.

Arinith moved up to the side of the Queen. Her guards even twitched at his approach. He frowned when he looked my way.

"I will not hold any of the others to their oath to me," I said, which seemed to surprise everyone, including Arinith. "I don't want anyone feeling an obligation to stand by me if they think that might cause them trouble. I know this will make the clan weaker, but I also understand there are far too many factors involved in this problem."

"And what do you want, Summerfield?" the Queen asked.

An easy one to answer.

"I want whatever is best for my friends. I don't want to see them suffer for a mistake I've made. How can I make this right?"

She tilted her head, eyes narrowed. Tessa's fingers tightened again, but when I dared a glance his way, he gave a nod that made me think I had said the right thing, dangerous though it might be.

"I cannot be certain you have done anything wrong," she admitted. That drew sounds from the crowd. No one was leaving now, and I had the feeling they all wanted to know how she was going to decide. I hadn't thought how this would affect them. A new clan? When was the last time they'd had a new clan? There was a matter I had never even considered.

"I am a problem, whether I intend it or not," I said.

"If you are not the one behind this, then you moved to protect me without any regard for your personal safety. Given that only you and one of my guards were wounded, I am starting to think you are the victim here and that you acted with concern only for others."

Oh yes, that drew startled sounds again. The shock of the attack had worn off, and the others were starting to see more of the situation.

"This is what he does," Tessa said. "Which makes it an honor to serve him ... but exceedingly frustrating at times."

Those words drew emphatic nods of agreement from Brandis, Kala, and York.

Queen Amata laughed and moved back to her throne. Others began to mill around, and music started a moment later, though quiet and subdued.

People watched us, but with far less anger than I had expected. I saw thoughtful nods from some and marked the clan colors -- mostly the golds of Dragon and the grays of Wolf. Had we won another group to our side? I couldn't be certain, and I wasn't going to ask the others right now.

"I need to rest. To sit down if we dare," I warned.

"We can go," Kala said.

"No. We aren't going to rush off right now as though we don't trust anyone."

"It's not safe here," Brandis said.

"I had noticed." I glanced at Vane who looked anxious

and unsettled still. "Stay with Vane. Keep him calm, Brandis. We don't want this worse."

He started to argue but then nodded to Kala to take his place. I saw how the Queen watched as Brandis crossed to Vane and put a hand on his arm. She looked pleased, I thought. No doubt no one wanted a half-grown, and more than a little untrained, Dragon Clan Totem changing again.

My people escorted me to the side of the room. I wasn't sure the chairs had been there before, but I didn't care if it was proper or not at this point. We were near the queen and her guards. None of them looked unhappy to have us there. Good. I sat down and tried to relax, despite being back on show again.

All my people were hanging close now, including Arinith. I gave him a nod.

"I'm serious about releasing anyone from their oath," I said aloud. "I know this might be trouble, but the rest of you have clans you can go back to, right? And Arinith doesn't even need a clan."

Arinith gave a quick nod and a glance at Queen Amata who was listening to us. No matter.

"I'll speak with each of the others about the situation," Tessa decided.

"Do you think you can do so without growling at them? I really don't think that's going to help a lot."

Queen Amata laughed first and then gave me a different look as she leaned our way.

"I think you should not make decisions too quickly, Summerfield," she said. "There is no reason to make hasty choices."

"I appreciate your concern," I said with a bow of my head. I almost let it stay there, too weary to continue. But I had something that needed to be said. "However, I know this can't be a good situation for the fae. I don't want to be the cause of trouble and change in your realm."

Something happened that startled both me and the rest of the room from the looks of things. Both the Queen and Tessa went very still, and I could tell from their faces that they were both having visions. I didn't know she had this power as well. I had thought it was a totem gift, but now I suspected Tessa was a rarity even in that rare company.

We all waited, music playing quietly in the background.

Queen Amata blinked first and looked at me with a bit more puzzlement than before.

"I think you may be a sign of the times, Summerfield," she said, and Tessa gave a slight nod as well. "I think, perhaps, we have reached an age of change."

Those words silenced everyone.

And I didn't ask.

CHAPTER 16

We stayed late, and I slept well that night. I don't think it was even Tessa's work. We were over halfway through the Fae Winter Court, and I had survived so far, though barely. I just had to make it through a couple more of the fae events and the family gathering. Was that tonight? I was losing track of time.

I got up a little past dawn. I couldn't tell if the weather was better or worse, and I didn't care. I showered and dressed. I could smell someone fixing breakfast, and I had to wonder if any of the fae slept these days. I felt sorry for them.

My people knew the morning routine.

"Tea is on," Tessa said as I came out of the bedroom. "Everything looks good this morning so far."

"Good," I said. I nodded to the others and went to the front door to pick up the newspaper Pablo had brought up dropped off there. Nice to keep some link to the real world. To *my* real world.

I glanced at the front page as I pushed the door closed.

Stopped.

Stared.

Summerfield Heir: Drugs and Cult

The byline was Brian Kenwood and Ted Jacobs.

I couldn't move. I couldn't read any farther than the

headline. All I could do was stare at those words and wonder why I had been so stupid not consider those two. My picture right there on the front page.

"Oh hell!"

Tessa came to the hallway at the same time that the phone began to ring. *Yellow Rose of Texas.* I took the steps to the kitchen and the phone where it had been charging.

I tossed the paper to Tessa. "That's Rose. I suggest all of you stay back because this could be dangerous."

Tessa stared at the paper in the same blank way I had a moment before.

I picked up the phone and put it to my ear and didn't even give her a chance to speak.

"I just saw, Rose," I said. "Did you see the names on the report? Send out the dogs of war. They've gone too far this time."

"Sunflower," she said. Then she stopped and took a deep breath. "I am going to hang them by their balls. I'm going to sue the paper. I'm going to --" She stopped again and took several deep breaths this time.

"None of this is true --"

"Of course, it isn't true!" she yelled, startled that I'd even say such a thing. I felt better to hear those words until I crossed to the table where Tessa had laid the paper out. More pictures of me. Tessa, too. His former occupation as a fortune teller had not gone unnoticed, nor the fact that we both worked at Woo Woo News. I saw some reference to a large mailing list, the implication that I used it for some reason. A picture of Julia.

I hadn't heard everything Rose said when the rage came

over me.

"I am putting all my people on this, and we will get an answer as to why the newspaper even listened to these two," she snarled, her voice rising again and getting my attention. "From what I can see of the story, it's all supposition, and there isn't a single bit of fact in there. This isn't normal. Is there anything else I should know about?"

I considered mentioning fae assassins and ancient gods, but this was probably not the best time. "One of my workers here told me that there were people in his old neighborhood spreading the word that I was dealing in drugs. I don't know why I never even considered Jacobs and Kenwood."

"Because you didn't think even they could be this stupid?" Rose asked.

"Maybe." I almost mentioned Lenz, but then I considered that someone might have the phones tapped and I didn't want to drag him into this if he had so far avoided detection.

"The report says the FBI is investigating," Rose said. I hadn't seen that part. "I can't believe that anyone has gone along with this!"

I grunted a reply, doing a quick scan of the rest of the report. It did seem rather weak on facts. They didn't mention the work we really did do, of course. They noted late night deliveries. They hinted at siege preparations. Oh yes, we were going to hold up here with two cases of fine champagne and the best Filet Mignon I could buy.

No, it didn't make sense.

Tessa and Brandis started to talk about war. I had to wave them to be quiet before Rose heard, though I had the feeling she might agree.

I had never seen Rose so upset before. Not angry -- irate. Every few moments she had to stop and take deep breaths and I remembered Dr. Penn, the family doctor, saying she had to start taking care of her blood pressure.

I suspected this was not the time to mention it to her.

"This is going to be trouble." Rose at least sounded a bit calmer now. "We will need to go over everything these two bastards might have, besides pictures of you not doing anything wrong. You need to cut your hair."

"No, I don't."

She laughed finally. "Yes, you're right. Okay. I'm heading over. We'll start going over everything."

I didn't even have time say yes, no, or good-bye before she hung up.

"Rose his heading over here. I suggest the rest of you find some place at a safe distance."

"This is not good," Tessa said, tapping the paper. "Why had we never considered these two in the scheme of other things?"

"I don't know," I admitted. "Except that we've had too many other things going on."

"Or someone subtly made certain we didn't look," Brandis replied. Tessa nodded agreement, and neither of them mentioned Gryn, though that would be our first guess.

"Tessa, lots of people are going to be looking into the foundation. Make certain we're up to date on all the paperwork."

He nodded. "I'll start spreading the word to the others in The Fortress, too. People are going to be upset."

"I'll help pay for anyone who wants to move," I said.

"This may well be more trouble than any of them want, especially with their children here."

He agreed with a bit of a snarl and started to turn -- but then he stopped, and his eyes went unfocused. I knew that look and waited, hoping that he saw something helpful.

A moment later he shook his head, still frowning. "I think there is someone outside with his hand in this. Someone manipulating things, Summerfield."

"Someone who might have manipulated the newspaper," I said, tapping the article.

That made sense since nothing in the story should have made it to press, let alone the front page. The FBI clearly didn't have anything on me. Had this person pulled the FBI in with magic?

"Gryn," I said. Tessa gave a tentative nod. "Gryn has been on this side long enough to know what would make trouble for me. We need to warn Julia --"

"I'll take care of it," Tessa said. "You think about how to deal quietly and sanely with your sister."

"Once she turns professional instead of sibling.... Well, I wouldn't want to be anyone in her path. Someone has made a serious mistake, Tessa, and it wasn't us."

Tessa suddenly grinned. "You're right. And that makes me think all the more that it must be someone from the other side. Gryn looks more likely again."

I scanned the paper. "The report makes a big deal that most of you do not have outside jobs and that quite a few hang around in Fontenelle Forest. We have that covered, at least, but make certain the others realize they're going to get asked about the work --"

"Like we have not been doing that work? Oh, not this week," Brandis said. "After all, we're all off for the holidays, right?"

"We will not mention giant lizards in Fontenelle Forest in any of our reports, right?"

"Right," Tessa agreed. He was already waving the others out.

They cleaned up after themselves, but Kala put a plate of food on the table for me before she headed out. I could see anger and distress in their faces and almost told them to calm down -- but no. Anyone in this situation would be mad.

Tessa asked Brandis to take care of his part while he remained. "I was in the picture, too. I can use that as an excuse for being here. We don't dare leave you entirely alone. I could become invisible, but I don't want to do that with your sister."

"Probably wise," I said. I sipped tea and ate my bacon and eggs. "This is all bogus. There is not a thing here that's true, but that doesn't mean people won't believe the implications, no matter what else we do."

"I suspect that might have been their plan from the start," Tessa said. "They have nothing that could really get you in trouble, but they are both set on ruining you."

I frowned, but then I pushed the paper away. "I have never worried about what others thought of me in the past. I'm not going to do so now. You know, it's possible that Gryn, if it is him, might even have had a hand in influencing Kenwood and Jacobs to take up this campaign against me, too. He would have needed people to do the work. Those two would have been easy to manipulate."

"Oh yes," Tessa agreed. He sipped his tea and frowned.

"Which makes turning the two of them into toads is bad Karma, I suppose."

"Yeah, that's the unfortunate part of having a conscious, you know."

"Gryn wouldn't be slow in using his powers to influence people into doing things they would not otherwise do. Kenwood and Jacobs are cowards on their own, but they would be easy to manipulate," Tessa said with a snarl. "The others, though -- the newspaper is the one part that is not what I would expect. They've always been careful about what they print. I think Gryn might have help."

"And you don't just mean Roan."

"Roan?" He laughed. "No, not him. We need to look deeper."

Rose arrived just after I had gotten a pot of coffee ready for her. She knocked on the door with a measured, even beat rather than just knocking it down and stomping in. I appreciated her patience.

"Tessa is here," I said, waving a hand toward the dining room where he sat on the phone with a very irate Julia. In fact, Julia might have even topped Rose, but Tessa was talking her down, little though he liked using phones.

"Good. Tessa seems to be listed almost as often as you in this travesty," she said and gave him a quick, professional nod. "I talked to some of the rest of the family. No one is happy about this, Sunflower."

"Should we cancel the party?" I asked, thinking about that problem for the first time.

"No. We are not going to indicate we believe you are involved in anything illegal," Rose emphatically replied as she took a chair at the table.

"But --"

"I talked to the grandparents. They are coming here whether you have a party or not tonight. I think the rest of us better show up as well, don't you think?"

I just waved my hands in resignation. I didn't know what we should do at this point.

"Let's talk about the rest of this. I get the feeling there must be far more than what the paper is listing or else the FBI wouldn't be involved."

We mostly discussed the ecology work, which seemed to be drawing the most attention. Tessa got my laptop, and I pulled up dozens of legit reports and dropped them onto a thumb drive for her. Then we went through the list of late-night deliveries, and I was able to tell her what every single one was, which mostly had to do with rebuilding part of The Fortress -- I managed not to call it that -- into a room for the gathering tonight. I even told her about building the castle for the kids.

"Well, damn, SB," she said, finally dropping Sunflower again for a while. I think I had just grown up in her eyes, which seemed very odd right then. "Yeah, some of this looks questionable, but none of it would look illegal after even a quick check. The only one that does is the withdrawal of $100,000 a few days ago, but they could have made that up --"

"No, that's real. I do it every year. I give it over to a guy at the utility department, and he takes care of the bills of people who have had a hard year. Cash so it can't be traced back to me."

Rose blinked several times. "Well, damn. If we have to,

we'll bring that one out, too, since it will be easy to trace."

I didn't like it, but I knew better than to argue with her.

She stood to leave and put a hand on my shoulder. "We'll get this figured out. Just don't do anything odd."

"Ah --"

"Yeah, forget that one. If you started acting normal now, people would know there is stuff going on."

I walked her back to the door. "You can talk to the others here --"

"Not today," she said and looked at her watch. "I have to start setting up our work plan on this one. You know, even if this weren't you, SB, we'd have jumped on a case like this. We are going to get this fixed."

"Thanks," I said and smiled, but we both knew that no matter what, some people were always going to believe the worst just because of who I was.

She patted my arm and walked back down the hall.

I went back to sit with Tessa. I read the report again and started making notes. We were going to have to answer the allegations, step by step.

"We are not going to be long at the fae gathering today," Tessa said. I frowned, but he looked adamant. "This is the middle of the Court. Many people take the day off. We'll do our duty, but we'll be back early. Tonight is your family gathering. We are going to do everything to make this one work right, Summerfield. Right now, we dare not be lax in anything."

I cursed. "I still haven't gotten presents for my sisters. Damn!"

"What sort of thing?"

"Too late," I said. "I don't dare go shopping. But I need something special."

"Something *magical*," Tessa said.

He moved his hands over the table and slowly shaped a glass rose of such perfect color and shape that the sight took my breath away.

"Oh yes, that will do perfectly. A flower for each of the five. And maybe a bouquet for my grandmother as well?"

Tessa smiled. "This problem, at least, is an easy fix."

"Jacobs, Kenwood -- Gryn -- they're all going to be surprised at how much of a mistake they made."

"Yes," Tessa said. "And I suspect Gryn should be worried about your sisters."

I smiled and thought about pointing them in his direction.

Oh yes, things looked much better.

CHAPTER 17

S tanley, my grandparent's butler, arrived an hour before the gathering to take up the position as the person at the door, bringing them in.

I gave him a heartfelt shake of the hand when he arrived, and he unexpectedly grinned. "You'll do fine, SB," he said, dropping formality since no other members of the family were there yet. We stepped into the lobby of The Fortress, which we had converted into a coat room, with Pam there to help. Pablo had the position at the door itself, and I had six other guys standing by to park cars in a nearby lot that I'd hired for the night. If anyone had to leave early, I had my Hummer and Mercedes ready for them.

The old van still sat on the street though they'd moved the vehicle after they got a ticket. I found that amusing on a day like this.

"We're bound to have reporters," I warned with a shake of my head. "I'm still not sure this is such a good idea, given the newspaper report --"

"Screw the newspaper report," Stanley said, so plainly spoken that I stared at him in shock. "And I'm looking forward to any reporter trying to get past me."

I tried to hide my surprise as I took him to the inner door and opened it to show him the main room.

He stopped in the doorway, shocked. "This is -- this is incredible!"

I knew we'd done an exceptional job, most of it in real world building rather than massive amounts of magic. The place did look lovely. The little touches of magic, which included flowers and lights, didn't hurt. The large pine tree at the end of the room would go back to the forest after we were done with him, too. I felt better for that one.

"This is gorgeous! I can't believe this was a garage!"

I hadn't expected Stanley to be so enthusiastic. He checked to make certain the settings at the tables were right. He checked the kitchen where the chef and his people were busy whipping up their own magic. Then back to the main room.

"I only see one problem, SB," he said, looking around again.

I looked as well, trying to figure out what we missed and if we could make it right in the next hour without magic which would be too obvious now --

"Don't panic," Stanley said and dropped a hand on my shoulder. "The only problem I see is that they're going to want to come back here every year."

"Ah. Oh. Damn. I don't think I could take this kind of pressure."

He laughed and patted me on the shoulder.

The reporters arrived before the guests, but they stayed across the street in the park. I waved a couple times. To hell with being worried about every little thing that might go wrong. So far, I had survived the Winter Court (granted with a few more scars), and the family gathering was not going to be nearly as bad.

Right. I could believe that until I saw my sisters, their husbands and their children all heading my way. I stood my ground, greeting them nicely and was the one to walk Rose into the room.

"Oh my God!"

She spun and hugged me.

Okay, I had not expected *that* reaction.

The rest of the family slowly arrived, most of them stunned, though Cousin Tommy sneered a bit, which was so typical for him that it settled my nerves.

The grandparents arrived amid all the others, and I went out to the car to escort Grandmother up to the building while grandfather followed behind. Cameras flashed, but they kept their distance.

"We're going to see those bastards pay, SB," Grandfather said with a pat on my shoulder.

Good to have the family on my side.

Grandma was so enchanted with the room that she wanted to talk to the designer. I sent Tessa and Kala her way before I checked the kitchen and found no trouble there, either.

York played his harp. Considering he had last played for the Queen of the Fae, this was quite an event, even though the others didn't realize it. They did appreciate the music, though.

Everything was going very well. Better than I had expected.

So, of course, Dagan showed up.

No one else saw him appear except for Brandis, though the other fae felt the intrusion. Since he was inside The

Fortress already, people automatically assumed he was one of my people.

I excused myself from talking to one of my cousins and walked over to deal with him. Tessa leapt to follow, moving a little too fast and might have drawn some attention except York started playing again. Brandis, coming from another direction, arrived almost ahead of us.

We reached the area to the side of the room where the elevators were hidden behind a screen.

I grabbed Dagan by the arm and pulled him out of sight. Even Tessa gave a yelp of surprise.

"I don't care who you are," I said, looking at Dagon. "I don't care what you can do. Wipe me off the face of the earth if that's what you intend. But you are not going to upset my grandparents and sisters while they are here."

"You cannot --"

"This is my place," I said, cutting him short. I think, maybe, I had not had enough sleep. A part of me shouted in my head that this was not the way I should be dealing with an Ancient God. I didn't listen. There was far too much piling up on me, and this was a problem I didn't need. "This is my place and my time, and the one thing I will not allow is for you to do something to upset the others."

"You think you can stop me," he said, his head tilted slightly.

He had a point there.

"I think -- I think I could *wish* for something to happen that might make it difficult for you. Shall we give it a try?"

Tessa had put a hand on my arm and was about to pull me away.

"You are only human."

"And this is a human world. Things have changed. This is not the time to deal with our problems, at least not if you don't intend to pull considerably more humans into the situation. Is that what you want? Because I can tell you right now, we've grown far past the *kneeling before an Ancient God* mode. You might find us a bit more trouble than you expect."

I think I had stumbled onto something there. Dagan blinked this time, which I had not seen him do. Then he disappeared.

Tessa grabbed me by the shoulder and spun me around.

"Are you crazy?"

"Yes. Totally insane, Tessa." I thought I ought to be shaking in reaction. I didn't have time. "I want the next three hours to go well. That's all I'm asking for tonight. Get this done and the family back out of here, and then we can deal with all the rest of this insanity. Right now, I want calm."

Tessa took a deeper breath. "You're right. Still, don't ever do something that stupid again. I've never known you to take such a risk."

"I needed to get his attention. He's confused about the world, Tessa. That might help us."

"We'll look into it. We're about to serve dinner. Presents with desert, right?"

"Right."

So, we went from dealing with an ancient god to making certain everyone's food was properly served.

And Tessa wondered why I was going more than a little crazy?

Dinner went exceptionally well, and that was entirely the

chef's work. He did magic all his own. Grandmother even called him to the table and thanked him personally, which had rarely happened, even though he'd often cooked at other family gatherings.

"The kitchen is a joy," the tall, black man said with the kind of euphoria most people reserved for their favorite football team. "Your grandson has done a fantastic job."

"Yes, yes, he has," Grandfather replied. He rarely took notice of such things. "This has been the most pleasant holiday party I can remember."

I feared Stanley was right and this would become an annual event. Yeah, the room was staying.

Grandmother looked at her watch, and I thought we might be running late --

"There should be a two more showing up soon, Sunflower," she said with a tap on my arm. "Latecomers, I fear."

"We'll manage," I said and tried to think about who wasn't here. I knew a few cousins, and such were off vacationing in warmer climes, but other than them, I couldn't think of anyone else.

The food tasted excellent, though. Everyone was happy.

About halfway through the main course, the latecomers showed up at the door, Stanley showing them in --

"Mom! Dad!"

I rushed towards them before I even fully realized I was moving.

"Sunflower!" Mom took the few steps to meet me, dad at her back.

They were, absolutely, the last people I expected to see

here. Dressed in blue jeans, sweatshirts, and parkas, they looked like a couple strangers who had wandered in off the street.

"We were heading back to Nepal for a year," Mom explained as we got them settled at the table. Tessa went off to find them food. "And thought we might stop by here and get acclimatized to colder weather for a few days. We've been in India for most of two months. This is quite a change. My, the food smells heavenly!"

"There are some pleasures of civilization," I said with a bright smile.

"And you appear to have adapted well," she said and gave Tessa a very odd look when he put the plate before her. She glanced at me --

And then she looked at Brandis and Kala. I saw dad, who was seated by grandfather and talking, do the same thing. Oh, yeah. My parents had a feel for the unusual. We were going to be discussing my companions later, I was sure.

No matter. We had a wonderful time. Dinner was great, desert was fantastic. Tessa brought out the boxes of gifts for grandmother and my sisters, and I wished I had something for my mother as well, though, she seemed too happy to care.

She wasn't born a Summerfield, but I had always thought she fit the mold better than my father, who was quiet and introspective. Mom fit in with her daughters and sitting here I realized how much the girls had picked up from her in attitude, even though I was the one who had spent most of my life with mom and dad. The daughters didn't let anything mundane stop them from finding the truth.

"These are lovely!" Grandmother exclaimed as she pulled

out the vase with the glass flowers. Tessa had added a sunflower in that one, and I grinned to see it. Nice touch. My sisters each got a bouquet of glass flowers in the style of their own names, and I don't think I'd ever seen the five of them look so stunned and pleased before.

Yeah, magic helped. We had pulled off the impossible, I realized. Despite everything that was going on, we'd managed to make this a perfect gathering. I grinned at Tessa who looked pleased.

Kala took the children to the corner by the tree for their own presents. York went with her, and the kids got remarkably quiet as the two of them told a story. They might have gotten their attention with a little magic, but that wasn't what held their interest now.

"I want to hire those two," Aster said. "I didn't think you could get the kids that quiet."

"Don't break the spell," I said with a grin that got an eye roll from Tessa.

Except for the moment with Dagan and a little bit of trouble from the pixies who had decided to plague my cousin Tommy, nothing went wrong. Tommy couldn't see them, of course. They didn't hurt him, but he was damned embarrassed by the time he left. I smiled. Tommy was not my favorite cousin.

I finally ushered everyone out, including my parents who were going to stay with the grandparents rather than open up their own house for just a couple days. Never mind that the house's caretakers were there.

I felt ready to collapse. Karma had granted me one good night in this mess. I went inside, told Pablo and Pam to get some rest, and went back into the dining hall. I collapsed in the first chair I found.

Tessa took the chair across from me. The place had already been cleaned up with the usual fae efficiency to get things done, all quick and neat.

I looked up at him. "Yes?"

"Your parents suspect something about the fae."

"Yes."

"Summerfield --"

"They have been very many places, Tessa. They've seen a lot of strange things, as have I. That's why I don't have any trouble with the fae part of the insanity. They are not a problem. We don't need to make them into trouble especially since we don't need more."

He started to speak and then nodded. If anything, Tessa looked more worn than me. "We need to start getting ready for the Winter Court."

I wanted to curse. I honestly wanted to curse. But I stood.

My phone went off. Glynis -- which surprised me.

"Glyn?" I said, hastily.

A moment's pause.

"This is Glynis's father, Mr. Summerfield. Let me get straight to the point. We've seen the newspaper reports --"

"None of it is true!"

"That's what Glynis says. However, we've asked her to stay away from you until this can be cleared up to our satisfaction. She will not be coming back to college after the holidays. This is the last time she will use this number. I trust you will be gentleman enough not to track her down until she's ready."

"Yes sir," I said, my voice almost trembling.

The phone went dead.

I stared at it a moment.

"Son of a bitch!" I tossed the phone. Tessa caught it and looked at me in shock.

I explained the situation.

"We'll make this right," Tessa said. "We'll get everything cleared up with Jacobs and Kenwood, and they are going to be on the backside of Karma on this one."

I looked at him, still glowering. "I should have called Glyn. Maybe --"

"Maybe," he agreed. "I suspect not. Once this went to the newspapers, you knew that it was going to have a bad impact."

"Yes, I know." I took several deep breaths and tried to force calm again. "Let's go get ready."

He frowned a little, as though he didn't trust my sudden calm and cooperation. I didn't trust my emotions either. I would get through the fae Winter Court because I had to do it for others.

But when we got back --

"We are going to deal with Jacobs and Kenwood," I said. "They are not going to keep bothering me, Pam, or anyone else who happens to be connected with me."

"I think that work is in the hands of your sisters," Tessa said and managed one quick smile. I could almost return it. "However, I think we can come up with something a bit more personal when the time comes."

"Good. Let's get ready. Two more days of this?"

"I think so." He ran a hand through his hair. "I'm starting to lose track of time. We got through this gathering tonight,

Summerfield. That was no small trick."

"I know. It went well." I looked back at the tree. "We need to get ready for The Fortress celebration, too. We promised the kids something special."

"The castle is done," he said, waving to the wall that hid that surprise still. We walked towards the elevators. No stairs tonight. No time and no strength. "Everything we need is there for all the little princesses and princes. I had not ever spent so much time with human children, you know. They believe in magic. I wonder why?"

"Because they haven't been beaten down by the non-magic, real world yet," I replied and leaned back as the elevator started upward.

"And you never were a part of that world either," Tessa said. He looked at me, head tilted slightly. "I think that explains a great deal, you know."

"Maybe so," I agreed. I tried not to think about Glynis and the present I had for her. She was my friend and my link back to the real world of humans.

Nothing I could do now. Oh, I could go track Glynis down. I could beg at her doorstep, but something told me that was exactly the wrong thing to do.

The elevator stopped. I didn't get out.

"Summerfield?"

"It's dangerous being around me," I said suddenly and focused on Tessa as we stepped out into the hall. "Right now, it's dangerous for very many reasons. Maybe what's happened isn't karma slapping me in the face: maybe karma is protecting her."

"Ah. Ah. We'd do our best to keep her safe, like all the

others who have come into our fold, but she isn't close, and that makes everything more difficult. You might be right, Summerfield. However, that means --"

"That means things are going to get worse," I said.

He gave a weary nod.

We went to get ready and face the trouble. I wondered if I had time for a shower.

CHAPTER 18

S o we went to the Winter Court, and this time we brought pizza with us, making Vane ecstatic. He had a chance to point out different kinds and to discuss his favorites -- something for the young Dragon Clan Totem to do that connected him with the other fae who had seemed a little worried about being around him.

"You're right," Brandis said, surprised. "This is going to help -- and the pizza looks popular. We've been worried that the wall was growing stronger between Vane and his people. It's good they realize he is still the same in many ways."

Tessa watched the gathering. "I've been a long time away from the fae myself."

"I don't mean to --"

"I have been here for a long time, Summerfield," he interrupted. "This is not a situation you have created."

Gryn was at the heart of Tessa's problems, and he had probably helped create the trouble for the Dragon Clan and Brandis as well. They would have the matter settled in their own way. All my people had been out talking to other clans and most likely gathering the information they needed.

Not my concern, I supposed. I had more than enough trouble of my own. If Queen Amata did not confirm me, then I wouldn't have any reason to worry about what happened in the fae lands. Really and truly not my problem.

I kept thinking about how Glynis would react to the Fae Winter Court. Practical Glynis who would never believe in magic.

"Summerfield," Arinith said, coming up beside me.

I gave him a proper, though belated, bow. He returned it and laughed. "I am still not used to doing that, you know."

"Feel free to skip the formality if it bothers you."

"You mean that," he said, and it was not a question.

"We are much in the same situation, you know. I'm no more used to being a Lord than you are in having one."

"True enough."

"Why haven't you asked to be released?"

He glanced at Kala and Tessa, and I thought he might not want to say anything in front of them. If so, he quickly he changed his mind.

"Something is not right," Arinith said. He stepped closer, his voice lowering. "You and your people have seen more of the trouble than most of the others. You are tied to it in many ways, but I think that's only because you are outside the normal world of the fae. There is something wrong."

"Something other than humans stepping in?" I said.

"Oh, you have not stepped in," he said and appeared startled by his own words. "You have not. You have taken a role and stand as a guardian against troubles in your own realm. I hadn't considered your position until now, but you have not created a new clan; you have drawn members from the other groups to serve you. They do so because they see a need. Is that not so, Brandis of Dragon Clan and Tessa of Cat Clan?"

"Oh yes, we saw the need," Tessa said, and Brandis nodded. "Though taking the oath to him was not planned."

Arinith gave a little laugh. "You did the right thing to break away from me at that time and place. There, I have said it. I was not aware of the circumstances, and because I dared not use my magic without creating more trouble, everything seemed dire and wrong to me. When I found fae there, I wanted to bring them to me, to learn everything before I made a decision."

"And I stood in your way."

"It seemed so at first. I learned better. You have done well, Lord Summerfield."

I had not expected those words from him. He bowed his head and walked away.

"Well, hell," Tessa mumbled. "Okay, so Arinith really is on our side. I could never be certain with him."

"Does that help?"

"It can't hurt. Arinith is akin to the Queen and might have more influence with her. Or might not. She makes her own decisions and always has. We can only wait."

I thought we would not have to wait long. I saw the signal to come to the throne. The others glanced my way, and I suspected everyone was ready for the decision. I was. I just wanted this done so I could move on to the *next* problem.

When had my life gotten this complicated? From the moment I picked up the Dragon Clan Key? I'd had a lot of strange in my life before that moment. I was starting to think that my entire life had led up to being here. Fae Lord or not, I was going to keep having odd things going on.

That was a comfort, really. I didn't want to change. I gave

a proper bow to Queen Amata and stood, waiting for her decision --

And the wall behind the throne began to crack.

"Trouble!" I shouted and waved a hand toward the wall. That probably should have gotten me killed since the others would have expected me to use magic and I was aiming vaguely at the queen. Lucky for me -- in an odd sort of way -- but this was not the only wall cracking. Fae began to yell, and I felt magic sweeping through the area.

Shadows moving. Black oozing from the crack.

I'd faced this kind of trouble before.

"Water!" I shouted. "Get water and use it to attack the shadows!"

Tessa already began doing so. The Queen and her guards looked uncertain, but I shouted for my people to protect her.

"Fine," Brandis said. "You stand there with her."

He shoved me closer to the throne. Queen Amata looked startled. I bowed. "My apologies. They are frantic. Careful!"

A glob of black came straight at her. I leapt in the way.

And that was all I remembered for a while. I came back awake gasping and in such pain that I could barely move.

Queen Amata held me in her arms.

Some fae had died. I looked frantically for my people, but I could hardly move. The Queen's Guard was in sight, at least, standing around us. They were fighting hard against the shadow creatures and other things I didn't recognize.

"We need out of here," Tessa said, daring to kneel by the two of us. "They've cut off all the others. We need --"

"To go back to my realm," I gasped.

Tessa shook his head, looking at Queen Amata and back

at me, panic growing.

"Bring her and her guards with us. Tessa, I don't think we can hold on here. Get back and close the gate."

"Damn. Hell." He ran a hand through his hair. "Your pardon, my queen. But --"

"But you think he makes sense," she said, her voice steady but filled with anger. "Except they are intent on getting him --"

"Not me," I corrected. I startled them both. "I have been a ploy all along. They started with attacks on me, but now they've attacked when I was near Queen Amata to make it look as though she's just caught in the trouble."

"I think he might be right," Brandis dared say. I had not seen him standing over us. He looked at Queen Amata. "Please, come with us. Away from here. I promise you will be safe."

She didn't even pause. "To Summerfield! Let's go!"

She was not the only one still on this side of the protection Brandis, and Tessa had put up.

They got me to my feet. I didn't think I could stay there, but if I didn't, then I put someone else in danger trying to keep me moving. I forced myself to pull free of Tessa. He gave me a wild, worried look.

"I'll keep him moving," Queen Amata said.

No one argued.

The attackers were going wild, but the rest of the fae were fighting in earnest now, and I don't know if they even noticed what we were doing. The leader of the Wolf Clan was with us, his arm bleeding, but that wasn't stopping him from fighting off something with a lot of limbs and claws. I didn't look too closely. I just moved and kept moving. Tessa would start to falter, I feared. He'd gone through hell before this, too. But just the same, he and Brandis kept pulling up ice and changing it to water and throwing it into the path of the shadows which were probably the most dangerous of the creatures.

I wanted to see that everyone else had gotten free. Instead, I kept forcing one step in front of the other. It seemed a long way to our hall and things were no better there. My companions were determined to get us to safety. We kept inching forward. I, at least, began to recover my breath.

I could see the tunnel ahead. We were going to be safe.

"Go!" Tessa waved to the opening. "We will hold them here. Start through. We're right behind you. Send the guards first, Queen Amata. Get everyone to the other side so Brandis, and I don't have to worry."

I thought she would argue. She had that look for a moment. I almost argued myself, but only because I didn't want to risk Tessa and Brandis as they stood the line.

We didn't argue. It was stupid to stand here and risk everyone's lives. But I looked back at the last moment --

"Take him," Queen Amata said and pushed me into Arinith's hold. "I can help."

"Dangerous --" Arinith began to protest. Then he looked at the wall of black ooze that my people were fighting back. "Be careful."

Queen Amata nodded. She moved to stand between Tessa and Brandis, and I thought they both must have been startled, but there was hardly a ripple in their magic.

"Be prepared," she said.

We all nodded. I was within a step of the tunnel.

"Now!"

She lifted her hands. Tessa and Brandis dropped their own magic. I hadn't expected that part.

I didn't expect the flood of water that swept straight into the black, either. It was as though she had opened up the Nile and swept it into the hall. I hoped the others beyond had a chance to get to safety --

"In the tunnel!" Tessa shouted. He grabbed me by the arm and all but threw me forward. I spun, but the others were there as well, and I retreated in haste to make room, turning to look at the other end of the tunnel and safety, at least for a moment.

Except we didn't get that far.

Dagan stepped between us and the exit. I swear I was about to leap forward and shake some sense into him when Tessa grabbed me back.

"You do not have the power to stop me, little human. You do not have power of your own --"

"But he has powerful friends," Tessa replied. It was all bluff. Tessa was on the verge of collapse and I didn't doubt Dagan could see it. Dagan smiled. He had not smiled before, and this was not a good new look for him.

He waved his hand.

And we were all somewhere else.

"Damn," I said and sat down in the sand. Hot day. I was already starting to feel too dry. We could get back --

Except before this, we'd gotten back because Brandis had a tie to Kala and could pull us to The Fortress. This time Brandis was here as well, and he didn't look happy.

"My apologies," I said, with a wave of my hand.

"You did not bring us here," the leader of the Wolf Clan

said.

"My problems, though," I said. "Another of my problems. Tessa? Brandis?"

"I have a link back to The Fortress," Brandis said. "Just give me a moment."

"This is where he brought us before," Kala said, looking around.

"His temple," I said, waving a hand towards the tell. I was too shaken to say more. "Tessa -- Brandis -- did we lose --"

"Our people moved quickly enough," Tessa said. He took a step closer and put a hand on my shoulder. "I don't know who else might have been lost. Queen Amata, I hope you realize that we had not meant to bring you here."

I had forgotten she was with us. I looked around with a start and would have fallen if Tessa hadn't put a hand on my shoulder. The Queen stood to my left, staring around with a frown, her guards keeping close.

"What is this?" she demanded.

"I -- I seem to have upset Dagan, the Ancient Assyrian God of Weather. He's been ... a problem."

"You have been dealing with an ancient god," she said, blinking several times. Surprised. I wasn't certain that was good.

"Not my choice and not me alone. Mostly not me at all. I apologize. Maybe we should have mentioned --"

"I would much rather be here than fighting off the shadows," she said. Her people nodded emphatically. "You fought them before. You gave the others the warning of how to fight them. Why?"

"Why wouldn't I?" I said, shocked by the idea.

And she nodded.

Lightning flashed across the sky. I struggled to my feet, knowing I did not dare look weak -- well, too weak -- when Dagan arrived.

"Show time," I mumbled. Tessa put a hand on my shoulder, sharing a little of his own energy. Not much. I feared we were all going to need to conserve.

Lightning came closer, fusing the sand before us in a blinding flash. I could feel the uncomfortable tingle up through my legs.

When the flash disappeared, Dagan stood before us. He'd grown taller, wider -- but even I could tell this was all illusion. That probably came from my time with the fae. I had a feel for magic these days.

I didn't even bow my head this time. He frowned.

"This is getting old," I said.

Tessa gave a little hiss of surprise.

"You dare --"

"Here's the problem, Dagan," I said. "You keep stepping in at appalling times. But the truth is, the way my life is going, you couldn't choose a good time. I have enemies everywhere. They may well settle this problem for us. If not, we can deal with the trouble between us in a few days."

"Summerfield," Tessa said, sounding panicked.

"We need to buy time to settle everything else," I said, looking at him.

I noted the Queen frowning so I might have annoyed her as well. Honestly, I was probably annoying everyone in two realms by this point.

I was tired. I hurt. I wanted to go home.

"You are a brave little human, but you cannot order me --
"

"Not an order," I began and saw his hand move. "Everyone down!"

The order got my people down fast. I think the Queen's people just knew enough to listen to me. Everyone dropped into the sand, and the threads of lightning flew over the top of us, close enough to be painful, but nothing more.

This was not working out --

"You think that's impressive?" Queen Amata said with a sound that came close to a purr. I had started to get back up, but I decided burrowing into the sand might be far, far wiser. I saw her move to my left, a woman in an elaborate gown that might have graced Queen Victoria's ballroom, standing in the middle of the scorching desert. She was not sweating. I was and I thought Tessa -- who had also not gotten up -- looked apprehensive.

The Queen walked forward and put herself in front of me. Oh Gods, that was not where I wanted anyone to stand with this rather annoyed God. This was not going to get better. On the other hand, if we were stuck here for a while, at least I could get out of the rest of Hell Week.

Lightning flashed again. I saw it spread outward around her and the rest of us.

"Pretty show," she said. "Let me try."

And we were suddenly in a blizzard.

I didn't have time to do more than yelp as Tessa grabbed my arm. The Queen and her people stepped through the fall of snowflakes. She smiled brightly.

"I don't dare do much more, not with the power I could

unleash here. Time to leave, I think. Brandis? You have the link?"

"Yes, Queen Amata," Brandis said. He looked pleased.

I could feel magic everywhere in the snow. I thought I heard Dagan yowl as the wind began to pick up.

We were already on our way again.

A different journey this time and I suspect that came from using some of the Queen's own power. Even though I could tell she was doing her best to be gentle, the power she unleashed tore through me. Chaos ruled everywhere, and into that chaos was a thread to which I tried to cling, to draw me back home.

I arrived back at The Fortress. The others had been there before me. I could tell because they were no longer dripping with melting snow. We were at the edge of the tunnel. I went back down on my knees.

"Summerfield," Tessa said and grabbed me up. "Praise all the gods -- except maybe Dagan -- that we got you back."

"What?" I didn't feel fully here.

"Dagan tried to grab you," Brandis replied. He leaned against the wall, gasping. I didn't want to think I had been lost --

Lost. That was the term. I frowned, feeling as though I might not really be fully here yet.

"Summerfield," Tessa said and shook me.

"Sorry, sorry," I said. "This is all madness. Everyone all right?"

"We're fine. Let's get up to the room."

"Get me steady first," I said. I trembled so much I couldn't stay on my feet without Tessa's help.

"Yes," he said. "Carefully, though. We need just to get you upstairs."

I felt him give me a little surge of power. It wasn't enough. He did so again, and that barely helped.

I saw Queen Amata looking at me oddly.

"I am sorry. Is there a problem?" I asked.

"You are more complicated than I thought, and your people far more loyal than I had expected. They would not let you go to the Chaos. They fought so hard that it gave me the power to get you back."

"Thank you," I said and bowed my head again, though I feared I would not be able to stand straight again. "Let's go."

CHAPTER 19

We stepped out into the ballroom and headed towards the elevators. No, we needed to take the stairs. I was not going to transport the Fae Queen and her guards anywhere in anything run by tech. Just not a good plan.

My people could carry me up --

Children. Laughing.

"Uncle Summerfield! Uncle Tessa! We went shopping!"

I heard a half dozen little voices echoing each other in English and Spanish. They rushed forward to tell us about their adventure and suddenly stopped. They were looking at Queen Amata in her extravagant gown with her guards.

"Who -- who are you?" Anita dared to ask, usually the shiest one of the group.

I looked back, frantic --

Queen Amata smiled softly and knelt before the children. "I am the Winter Queen. I've come for a visit."

"Oh," the children said, almost as one. Enchanted. I saw Pam and Rosa looking on with bemusement and confusion, though. I wasn't certain how I was going to talk my way around this one.

"Are you here for the holidays? Uncle Summerfield said we are going to have a party all our own. Will you come?"

"I would be delighted," she said, and she meant those words. I tried not to think this would be another problem --

A heartbeat later I heard a far different problem. A shout and other shouts. Shots --

"Into the elevator. Now!" I pushed children that way. I think Tessa understood faster than the others did and seemed to sweep them up, along with the two mothers.

We were not fast enough. The gunmen rushed into the room, wearing masks and carrying the kinds of weapons you hoped only to see on shows.

I moved away from the elevator doors when I saw one of the people take aim straight towards the crying children.

I leapt at him.

Oh yes, all hell broke loose. Tessa and Brandis yelled my name. Children screamed. Another set of people rushed in -- no masks. I heard them shout FBI --

I had counted on the magic to save me. It did, mostly. I felt Tessa's magic sweep out in a fan that knocked bullets aside. Unfortunately, this wasn't the only person firing. Something hit me in the leg with the kind of shock that you know is going to be worse in the next breath. I felt other magic as well. Quick, powerful --

Yes, the Queen was getting a dramatic introduction to my life.

I went straight down in a heap on the floor. My leg felt on fire, and I could feel a line of pain on my right arm. Everything moved around me, and I didn't think being helpless on the ground was going to be safe for long.

More shots.

And then quiet. Deathly quiet. I started to turn, but Tessa

and Brandis were already there. So was another man with a gun in his hand, which nearly got Tessa moving --

"FBI," the man said and held out a badge. "Put pressure on that wound and slow the bleeding. I have an ambulance already on the way."

Hell. I looked at Tessa and gave a little nod. We could not hide this wound, and there was no way he could now use magic to heal me. We were stuck in my world, and I was going to suffer for it.

Brandis was irate, though. "What the hell is going on!"

"We thought they were more of your people," he said. The FBI man kept talking, but I really didn't hear much after that. Damn. This just was not going to go well at all.

I happened to see the Queen, her face pale and her eyes blazing.

Oh, not good at all.

"Tessa," I whispered, and he leaned closer. The FBI man frowned and stayed close. "Get Queen Amata out of here. Don't let them take her in for questioning. Do something drastic. Order everyone but you to keep her safe. You come with me."

He looked back at the Queen and nodded. "We'll manage it. I've eased a little of the bleeding. That will help. Damn, Summerfield --"

He couldn't say much more. Police, FBI, and the ambulance had arrived. We had pandemonium in the room. I closed my eyes --

And I woke up in the hospital. I was uncomfortably lucid, which I suspected came from magic. The FBI man stood close by, and so did Tessa and a couple nurses.

"I didn't catch your name," I said.

Most of the people in the room jumped at the sound of my voice, though Tessa did not, which told me I was right about the magic.

The FBI man turned and took a couple steps to the bed, looking at readings which he seemed to understand. He turned back at me and gave a quick nod.

"I'm Agent Krig," he finally said. "And an apology hardly seems enough. We thought the young men coming into your building were more of your own workers until we saw one of them take out a gun and shoot the guy at the door --"

"Pablo!" I said and started to sit up, machinery screaming everywhere.

"Careful! Careful!" one of the nurses shoved me back down. Hard.

"He's fine, Summerfield," Tessa said. "I checked on him myself. A minor wound. They bandaged him up, and I sent him back home already." I looked at Tessa, wondering if he told me the truth. He gave that damned Cheshire Cat smile of his. "You don't trust me?" he asked.

"I'll consider it," I replied and looked back at Krig. "Who were they? Do you know yet?"

"Just started getting the info in when we arrived here. They're henchmen for a top drug lord. You want to guess which one?"

"I'd have to know names to guess," I said. Krig frowned. "I am not a drug lord. I resent that you have been taken in by Jacobs and Kenwood, and I want to know how the hell they lied so well that the FBI believed them."

"You know those two names."

"And you know why. Jacobs used to work with me. No, I take that back. The stupid bastard sat in a chair in the same office; he did not work. Pam, his soon-to-be ex-wife, now works for Woo Woo News instead. It was a good trade."

"Because you like Pam."

"Pam is a good friend. Even if she were more, which she isn't, that wouldn't excuse Jacobs' lies."

"And Kenwood?"

"He and Jacobs ought to be very happy together," I muttered and moved, fighting back a hiss of pain. My leg wasn't nearly numb enough. "You must have looked into their backgrounds. Why the hell are you listening to them?"

He gave me a hard stare, and I realized I needed to back up a bit. I was annoyed. I was worried. Tessa looked calm, though, so I had to believe that everything had gone relatively all right.

"It isn't my choice on where the FBI sends me," Krig said suddenly, and it almost sounded like an apology. "And you have to admit that things do look odd on your end."

"Odd is not a crime. What do I need to do to at least get you people to back off?"

He stood there for a moment, surprised by my words. I thought he was going to say something, but Dr. Penn came in, shaking his head and holding up a chart.

"You got here fast," I said.

"I was already here, kid. You got damned lucky. What the hell is going on?"

"Way too much purposeful misinformation in the world," I said. "How is my leg?"

"Good to go," he said. "The bullet missed the bone and

any major arteries. You're going to be sore for a while, but that's it."

"I can leave?"

"Yes," he said with a sigh. "I know. You want out of here before your sisters show up." He turned his attention to Krig. "You're the FBI person, right? I suggest you get this figured out and fast. You don't want the Unholy Five pissed at you, too."

Then he turned and left again. I was already starting to sit up, and Tessa moved to help me. They'd cut away my pant leg, but otherwise, I was still dressed. Good.

"Shoes?" I asked, looking around.

Krig looked ready to argue. I waved my hand. "Sisters coming. No time to mess around."

That got Tessa moving. I suspected he feared running up against my sisters more than he feared dealing with the Queen. Krig still looked ready to argue, though.

"What do you want?" I asked him. "What can I do to help prove this case against me is bogus?"

"Let us search the apartment building."

"Fine. Let's go."

"Now. You'll just let us in, without a court order --"

"Yes. I have nothing to hide, Krig. Let's go and at least get this part over so that we don't waste the court's time with you trying to get permission when I'll just let you come in. I'll talk to the rest of my people there and convince them to let you search their apartments. Do remember that we have children around, though."

"Yes," he said. "Okay. You two ride with me so I know you haven't sent word on ahead."

I nodded. Tessa didn't argue. He helped me get my shoes on, and Dr. Penn came back, peeking in the door.

"Run -- well, hobble -- while you can. Aster just pulled in."

"Let's go," I said.

Tessa had me out in the hall before Krig caught up with us. "You don't like your sisters?" he finally asked.

"I adore my sisters, but they think they need to run my life. You really don't want to deal with them tonight, Krig. Trust me."

"I've read a great deal about your family," he said.

"And?"

"We better move faster."

Krig, I decided, was a very smart FBI man. Tessa scored me a wheelchair. Dr. Penn brought my paperwork, and I was signed out as we headed down the hall. Aster rush passed us heading for ER, but she didn't expect to find me heading out. Tessa and Krig stood in front of me, and she never saw me.

I felt bad, to be honest. Aster looked worried. However, before we were fully out the door, I heard a familiar yell.

"He's going to drive me crazy!"

"Oh, we don't want to be caught now," I warned.

Tessa laughed as he helped me into the car, a touch of magic easing the pain in my leg.

Aster came to the door as we pulled away. I waved and saw her throw her hands up into the air in pure, unadulterated frustration.

"You do live dangerously after all," Krig said as he drove away.

"Just get us to the apartment before she can catch up with

us or send Rose," I warned.

"I expect neither of you to try and contact anyone before we get there. I have my people on the way. We'll do this clean and neat, and then we'll talk about why you've been set up."

Well, good.

I sat back and tried not think about turning my fae loose on Jacobs, Kenwood and any number of drug lords in this city. Why stop there? I could wipe out evil everywhere.

Yeah, now there was a plan sure to be rife with the kind of future I didn't want to think about. Sunflower Breeze Summerfield, savior of the universe. I could hear Queen playing the Flash Gordon music now.

Must have been the drugs.

We reached the apartment without any trouble. Pablo was at the door and rushed out to help me in as I hobbled along with Tessa's help.

"Summerfield! *Gracias A Dios!* You are safe! There has been such worry here! The children are upset. Everyone is upset!"

"I'm fine, fine -- how are you?"

"Worse in the last knife fight with the Black Knights," he said, waving it off. "What is happening?"

I put a hand on his arm, knowing he wasn't going to like this. "This is Agent Krig of the FBI --" Pablo's eyes flashed in a way I hadn't seen since he left his old neighborhood. "He's going to help prove I am not a drug lord."

"Ah. *Es veradad?* We can trust him?"

"Yes." I looked back to see more people coming up the walkway. "Tell me these are your people before I get very, very nervous --"

"Mine!" Krig said with an emphatic nod.

So, we made him nervous, too. Good, then. I didn't want to think this was all on one side.

I, of course, had other things to worry about. Ancient Assyrian Gods. Fae Queens and her guards. Those sorts of things.

We made a plan, the group of us standing there in the lobby. I would personally take them on the tour. They could go anywhere and look at anything, as long as they didn't frighten the children. They'd brought two dogs to sniff out drugs, and they all looked quite solemn about the work.

We started in the dining hall, where there was still some sign of the troubles. I saw blood on the rug and grimaced, knowing it was mine.

"We'll have it cleaned tomorrow," Tessa said. "And replace anything broken so we can have the apartment gathering without any trouble."

"Good. We need to do something special for the kids, though."

He nodded.

Krig looked at me, head tilted.

"Not a cult," I said. "But a lot of these people have come here from unfortunate circumstances. I want them to continue to feel safe. I don't want the children to think there is no hope of anything better. That never leads to a good life."

He gave a tentative nod, but I didn't think he looked very reassured. That was probably the normal state for FBI agents, though.

His people went through the room looking for hidden panels, checking the floor, looking behind the tree. We even opened and resealed packages. This was going to be a long, long night.

Then we went to look at the castle.

"It's all but done. A surprise for the kids so they have a place to play during the winter."

And on and on, through apartments where I at least got to sit down. Some of the people were not happy, but they calmed when I said this was the best idea. I got to see the kids and even played games with a few to pass the time.

I did have to field calls from my sisters. Rose started out irate that I had brought the FBI in, but then she changed her mind and decided cooperation was the far wiser choice in this mess.

"You have dangerous people after you, Sunflower. It's good if you can make the FBI your allies. That should help get this all settled properly."

"Aside from the fact that it's all lies, of course," I said with a slight laugh.

"Well yes, of course," she said and was not joking. "Take care."

"That should be the last of them unless I hear from my grandparents or my parents," I said, putting the phone back away. Krig had listened in and gave a nod.

"Your parents are in town."

"Yes. I haven't seen them in years. They've been -- oh, a lot of places, I suppose" I said.

"I read about your childhood."

I grinned, and he gave a little laugh.

The rest I had at the apartments had helped, but by the time we got to the upper floor and my apartment, I was tired and ready for this charade to end.

I had forgotten my guest, the Queen of the Fae. She sat on the sofa looking quite regal when we came in, though dressed in more appropriate clothing.

"This is Amata Court," Tessa said, with a nod to the woman. "We hired her to play a Winter Fairy for the children, and she had just made her first appearance when the others broke in."

Krig didn't question it -- a little magic, I supposed, to cover the fact they would not have seen her come inside the building.

Brandis and Kala were here, too. Lucky for me that Vane was not around for any of this insanity. I feared what would have happened if he'd been present at the shooting. Tessa was unsettled enough that I half expected him to turn cat on me.

"We are not going to find anything," Krig said while his people began to search through all the rooms. "It is plain there are no drug labs here, and all the supplies you brought in have been for legitimate reasons. That brings us to Kenwood and Jacobs."

I was the one who snarled at those names. I surprised Krig, but I waved away my own bad mood and went to sit in a chair by the table. Tessa went to make tea. I really just wanted to go get some sleep because drugs and blood loss were starting to work on me, despite the little bits of fae magic that had been helping.

"They have both crossed the line," I said as Krig pulled a chair out across from me, leaving the work in the apartment to his people. I did see the way he glanced around and came to grips with the idea I was rich. That must have gotten lost somewhere in the mess. The fae didn't know how much the paintings on my wall were worth, but Krig had a good idea. "Kenwood and I crossed a few paths on stories. He thinks he's a hotshot and when I turned down a byline with him, he took it personally. Which is good, since it was personal."

"And Jacobs says you are behind his divorce and that you are a cult leader, drugging your people, and planning a war."

"Pam needed a better place to live. It's closer to work and safer for her daughters."

"And that's why you do these things."

"Yes."

He blinked. "You mean that."

"Yes."

We sat in silence while as he looked around the room again, heard reports from his people.

"I think we are done here," Krig said and stood. "We will still be around keeping an eye on things. There are still some questions -- but not today. Get some rest."

I watched the group leave the room. Tessa sealed the door. Brandis moved out to the balcony and waited, hidden from the view by the shield.

"They all left. I thought we would be in the clear after they searched, but it sounded as though that's not entirely true," Brandis said, coming back in.

"Not entirely," I agreed. "But we're better off now than we had been. I need to rest. I really do, or I am going to fall over asleep right here. I apologize Queen Amata --"

"Get rest, Summerfield," she said. "My people and I have things to discuss."

I tried not to take that as a personal affront as I hobbled

to my room. When I looked back, Tessa gave me a little shrug, but he didn't look worried. Neither did Brandis or Kala.

"The Winter Court --" I said as I paused by the door to my room.

"We're taking care of everything," Tessa replied. "Trust us."

I did, of course. I went into the room, kicked off my shoes and carefully crawled in under the blankets. I did not even attempt to get out of my clothing, not the way things had been going these days.

I fell asleep almost immediately; the deep, dark sleep of the righteous.

CHAPTER 20

I woke the next morning with my leg aching and my head pounding. I peeled out of the clothing from the night before, grimacing at spots of blood. A shower didn't really help much.

I was not in a good mood when I came out of the room. I could see Tessa and Brandis at the table, and someone was in the kitchen, cooking.

I came around the corner to find my mother standing over the stove.

"Oh! Someone should have told me you were here!"

"Don't be silly," she said and waved a spatula in my direction. "Sit down. How are you? And how long have you been working with the fae?"

We all froze. All of us. Tessa didn't even blink. I didn't move from one step to the next. Brandis stared.

"Go sit down! You need to get off that leg. A shame the FBI people know about the wound or else you could have it gone by now. Do you still like your eggs scrambled?"

"Scrambled," I repeated, not really understanding the word as I went to the table and sat down.

"Good, good." She puttered around the kitchen, while we stared. It was a wonder to have her here, and I tried to latch on to that part and not think about the rest. She was my height, lean, and wore her slightly graying hair in braids. She wlue jeans, a sweatshirt with the sleeves pulled up. I just watched.

Soon she brought pancakes, eggs, sausage, and tea to the table. We were all three staring still.

"Dig in, dig in." She waved her hand at the food and began to ladle things to her own plate. "Your father is spending the morning with his parents. I begged off to spend a little quality time with my son. So how did you meet the fae? What clan are your friends from?"

So, she didn't know everything. I felt absurdly happy about that part.

"Last summer we had some trouble," I said and finally started grabbing food of my own.

"Oh yes. All those odd storms. I had sensed strange things going on. I called your sister -- probably not wise. They never made that connection that you had."

I decided not to go into details about trolls and such. Not just yet. Maybe after I stuffed myself on this good food.

"This is Tessa, the Cat Clan Totem and Brandis, the Dragon Clan Warlord."

She stopped eating and stared in shock. I had forgotten that Cat Clan and Dragon Clan were mortal enemies not so long ago.

I let Tessa and Brandis explain everything while I ate enough to almost make myself sick. I was content afterward, though.

"So now we're dealing with the Winter Court," Brandis said. "Which is going far better than we had hoped, although the Queen hasn't confirmed Summerfield's status yet."

"Ah. That is bothersome," my mother said with a frown. Then she lifted a hand again before Tessa or Brandis could say more. "I met a group of fae a few years ago. Wolf Clan, actually, up in the Alps. We spent several weeks sharing a camp. I have met many interesting people through the years. I never expected to meet more fae, though -- and certainly not a totem. I'm honored."

Tessa gave a little laugh. "I work with your son at Woo Woo News, Mrs. Summerfield. I don't think you need to be too honored at this point."

"I'm Maggie. Mrs. Summerfield is my mother-in-law," she replied and smiled. "I'll get the dishes --"

"Don't be silly," Tessa said and gave a wave of his hand.

Dishes swept through the air, cleaning while they moved, and went back into the cupboards.

"Well, that has to be handy," she said.

"Show off," I accused.

Tessa grinned. He patted Brandis on the shoulder and stood. "We're going to take care of some business at the Court and make certain everything is ready for tonight. This is the last night of the Winter Court and the Queen would like it to come off without a major problem."

"Be careful. Be damned careful out there," I said. "Any word on how the shadows got into the court yesterday?"

"Our friends the Dvergar had a hand in it," Brandis replied as he stood. "Everyone is looking into how they got there. The rest of the fae are anxious to have Queen Amata back, too."

"She's still here?"

"Yes. The Queen's guards suggested she stay until we all

return. Not everyone is happy about the decision and not everyone is convinced you weren't behind the entire thing."

"And she is still staying here?" I asked.

"She's convinced of your innocence," Brandis said. "And so are her guards."

Well, that was something. The two left, and I looked over at my mother who was frowning slightly --

"I know. It's all very odd," I said.

"Odd?" she asked, startled. "Oh, you mean the Fae. Oh yes, odd enough. I was just wondering if the weather was going to hold up for a couple more days before we head out again."

"The fae are here. I have the Assyrian God of Weather pissed at me. I am kind of thinking good weather isn't something to count on."

"You seem happy."

I smiled despite myself. "There are aspects of this that are fun. Some not so much. But I am helping others. I don't know how this is going to turn out, but it won't go badly just because I'm turning my back on what is needed."

"How can I help?"

"Keep your daughters occupied for the next twenty-four hours. Let me have peace on at least one front."

She gave a short laugh. "Well, it might be interesting."

"Do it as a study of another culture."

"So, is that how you manage in all this?" she said with a wave of her hand towards the apartment.

"Oh yes. This, the fae world, and all the rest," I said with a nod. "And it is fascinating, but you know that part."

She smiled and sat down with two cups of tea. We talked

for a while about the places we'd been, what we'd done -- my work both here and in the fae world.

"I'm glad to know one of the family is carrying on our commitment to strangeness," she said, giving me a hug as she headed out the door for lunch with dad and some of the family. "You be careful. And I'll snare your sisters for the afternoon. I can't promise to hold their interest for any longer, though."

"The afternoon would be wonderful," I agreed.

"And dinner," she added. "I'll rope your father into that one, too. Oh yes, this should be interesting."

She looked pleased as she left. I knew she loved her daughters, but quite honestly, they lived in different worlds.

Not long after she left, Tessa, Brandis, and Kala returned.

"We've called for the final Winter Court at the Queen's instructions. I'm going to seal up your leg wound and stop the pain, but I don't dare heal it since you're going to have to go back to your doctor. Just be damned careful."

I nodded. This was the final show. I had no idea how the Fae Queen would decide on my role as Lord Summerfield. I wasn't sure how much I should worry. I just wanted all of us to survive.

We dressed for the party. I had to admit that I was pleased we had made it this far. I didn't know what was going to happen tonight and from the looks on the faces of my people, neither did they.

We met up with the Queen at the castle. She looked it over with a little smile.

"For the children," I said as we went inside.

"So, they tell me. I eased the shock of the incident for the young ones, Summerfield."

"Thank you." I bowed my head and looked at my people. "Let's do this."

Tessa uncovered the portal he'd closed when we came scurrying through the last time. The way looked bright, clean, and safe. I didn't trust it, and neither did any of my people. They went in with the Queen's Guard and lined the ten-step path so that the Queen and I hurried through and out into the ice palace. We didn't wait in the hall since someone had been there watching for us, and word was already spreading that the Queen had returned.

They'd repaired most of the main room, at least. I hadn't asked about whom had died in the attack and regretted that omission. We crossed the room and to the throne without any trouble. Arinith moved straight to Queen Amata and gave a bow of his head.

"I have learned what you sent me to check on," he said, and loud enough that everyone heard.

"And?" the Queen said.

"It is as we suspected."

She gave a grim-faced nod and then turned my way. "Summerfield?"

Tessa looked close to panic as he walked with me, Brandis at my other side. I would rather they hadn't gone along, but there was no use trying to save them. And they might, yet, save me.

Everyone fell silent.

"Tell us what you learned, Arinith."

He gave a bow of this head. "I observed the person without him or his allies knowing. I made note of their movements and their connections, and I have confirmed the worse. They are the ones who set this trouble in motion, and they are, indeed, trying to kill you, Queen Amata."

I frowned. A lot of people looked as though they thought this was about us, but I knew better. Tessa and Brandis both shifted slightly, but I gave them both looks and signaled calm.

The Queen stood as others began to whisper, the sound spreading through the room.

"The Winter Court has been plagued with trouble," she said, drawing silence from everyone. "We have been witness to attempts that would undermine the world of the fae -- and they were not done by Summerfield."

Even I gave a sigh of relief.

"Gryn, the former warlord of the Cat Clan, is declared a traitor to all fae. I suspect he has already run, hasn't he? Roan, the totem of the Centaur Clan, has been implicated as well, though I suspect he has been led astray by Gryn since he is not known for making decisions on his own. I put him in the hands of his clan leader and warlord, and if they cannot control him, I shall know why. If there is more trouble from him, I will deal with him personally."

Roan was a coward. Even I knew it. I suspected that her threat was going to be enough to keep him in line for a long, long time.

She went up the steps to her throne and then turned around to look out at us. "Summerfield."

I stepped closer and gave a bow.

"You are not one of us."

"No, I am not," I said. "And I know this is a problem."

"You stepped in and did your best to save me -- and I let

you, to see how you might handle the matter."

I smiled because I had wondered how someone so powerful as the Queen could be helpless. I hadn't asked, for fear I was stepping over the line.

"And while you maintained your own innocence, you did not point the finger at Gryn, not during the time I stayed in your realm where you might have taken advantage of my presence to plead your own case, both against Gryn and as Lord of the human world."

"I felt it better if you observed matters without my interference."

"Perhaps he has driven Gryn to this situation," someone said behind me. I didn't turn to look.

"The trouble with the Dragon Clan and the Cat Clan both happened because of Gryn, and long before I was involved," I reminded everyone.

Queen Amata nodded agreement. "I went to your world to see this place where I have not gone for a while." I winced. I suspected others saw as well. The Queen leaned closer to me, though, and no one dared speak. "You live in a dark and dangerous world, and yet in the midst of this madness, you have created a place of wonder and safety for both your fae and your human friends. This is how it should be. I confirm you in your position as Lord Summerfield. I hope that you may spread such wonder and safety to others of your kind."

"Thank you, my Queen," I said and bowed.

"And now -- and now --" She looked around. "I do hope there is more pizza."

My people were ecstatic. More so than I expected, and I think that might have infected the others. We had a good evening, really. And lots of pizza.

I could tell everyone was glad just to have the matter settled. My people -- really mine now -- were not the only ones who seemed happy, either. Maybe that had more to do with Gryn and Roan, though. Those two couldn't have been the most popular people in the fae lands, even before this current trouble.

I did wonder where Gryn had gone and when we were going to be dealing with him again.

I danced with Kala, too.

"At least that trouble is now over," she said as we took to the dance floor with other fae.

"Over?" I said. "I am now *Lord Summerfield*. I think our trouble has just barely begun."

"True enough." But she still looked happy, which made me think the alternative of me not being Lord Summerfield must have been much worse. I didn't ask. I didn't need to think about 'what if' when we had more than enough trouble with the current situation.

None of us mentioned Dagan who was not going to be happy to learn I had been confirmed in my position.

Oh yes. Trouble still coming.

However, the last night of the Winter Court went well. No one dared make trouble, and I think anyone who was not happy at having a human among the nobility knew enough not to say anything right now.

The time for the last dance came and I waltzed with the Queen again. I can't say I was sorry to have the Winter Court over. I bowed to her as the music died.

She went to her throne and stood before it. "Go to your

places. Find peace in your world."

Everyone bowed. The Queen signaled her people, and they made their way out of the room. As soon as she was gone, the rest of us began to head for our own exits.

"Dagan is bound to have picked up on what happened," I said to Tessa as we neared the tunnel. All of my people were with me, including Arinith and Vane as well. "This is going to be dangerous, I fear."

"We'll be quick." Tessa looked back behind us. "Everyone is out. Bring it down."

I looked back to see the lovely ice palace melting back into the ground. No one looked particularly sorry to see it going, probably because we had all barely survived. Still, it had been a lovely place and they'd done a fantastic job.

And I was Lord Summerfield. I still wasn't certain what that would mean. Trouble, of course; we had already figured that out. But I needed to learn more of my responsibilities.

Right. A whole new career move from the top reporter for Woo Woo News.

"Let's go," Tessa said. He took hold of my arm.

We rushed forward. I felt something start to tug at me, but Tessa growled -- sure wish he wouldn't do that -- and Brandis shouted something. Whatever had hold of me lost the touch, and we went through with all the others.

Safe at home, more or less.

"Out of these clothes," I said, worried about who we might show up this time. "And unfix the leg."

Tessa did so, switching clothing with magic and removing the magic on my wound. I managed not to curse at the sudden pain. He also handed me a cane, which at least helped.

We made it all the way to the elevators before anyone came into the area. Most of the others had gone up the stairs, so at least it didn't look so odd to have Tessa, Brandis and I standing there.

I gave Pablo a quick smile. He gave us an odd look, though.

"I came down to see how much work we needed to do before Christmas Eve," I said, waving towards the main room. "Everything looks good."

"We fix," Pablo agreed. "The FBI people -- they called because no one answering upstairs. Say they are coming over."

"Of course, they are," I said. I couldn't get five minutes of calm. I turned away from the elevator and went to the closest table and chairs. "Let them in when they arrive, Pablo."

He gave a worried nod and headed back to the door. I suspected the idea that the FBI were hanging around bothered him more than he would say.

I had to wonder about the newest problem. Unfortunately, being Lord Summerfield was not going to help.

CHAPTER 21

B randis went on up to tell the others what was going on, so they didn't worry. He could have done so with magic, but he must have realized that having him glowering at the FBI would not help our situation. I sat down, happy to be off my feet again, to be honest. My leg ached. I was not in a good and benevolent mood towards drug dealers and gun merchants right at this moment.

We didn't have long to wait. In a few minutes they arrived, and they were not alone. I recognized four of the FBI agents, including Krig. They brought four local cops -- none of them Lenz -- someone from the city council, and someone who was high up on the newspaper, too.

They also brought Kenwood and Jacobs.

Well, this looked like a good show. Kenwood and Jacobs appeared smug, but from the look on Krig's face, I didn't think that would last for long.

"As I told all these people, this is an unofficial meeting to discuss certain matters in the Summerfield case. What goes on here is not for publication."

Everyone nodded, but Kenwood got a sly grin and put his hand in his pocket. Did he really think he was fooling anyone?

"Yesterday, after the unfortunate shooting incident, Mr.

Summerfield gave the FBI full permission to search every inch of this apartment building for drugs, drug-making equipment, cult activities, guns and any other sign of the trouble which Mr. Kenwood and Mr. Jacobs named in their report. We found no sign of any such items anywhere."

Mr. Newspaper man winced and paled. Oh yes, after that report appeared front page, he had to be worried about what I was going to do about the slander.

"Must have cleared it out after the report," Jacobs said and looked at me, daring me to say otherwise or to get irate.

I didn't. At least not so Jacobs would notice, though the little weasel was working his way up to another good dose of Karma, I thought.

"Well, even if that happened, Mr. Jacobs, I would consider it the fault of you and your colleges for releasing the story before we were done with the investigation."

"We are looking into why the story made it to the paper," Mr. Newspaperman said. He had started to perspire. "Even before tonight, we were trying to figure out how this happened. The story should never have --"

I lifted my hand. He went quiet. "I am sure we'll all be looking into what happened, but unless I learn there was complicity of the newspaper with Kenwood and Jacobs, I don't believe you need worry about a lawsuit."

"Thank you. I assure you that no one of any rank at the paper had any part in this travesty.

Jacobs was getting angry. "He must have taken --"

"As it happens, since the FBI was already watching the building, we know for a fact that nothing was taken out. So, it appears that Kenwood and Jacobs were purposely trying to create a difficult situation for Mr. Summerfield."

"Sunflower is into the bad stuff," Jacobs said. "I know he is. Remember, I've been in the building. I know what I saw."

"Then you had better take us to the location, Mr. Jacobs," Krig said.

"Oh, he's moved everything out. You said so. But I know --"

"If there was something in the building, like the meth lab you described to us, then there will still be traces. Put up or shut up, Jacobs, because you are slipping fast into areas that I don't think you want to go with me."

Jacobs opened his mouth. I really thought he was going to take that next step. He did not.

"We still had one item on you, Summerfield, that was troublesome. We knew that you had withdrawn a large amount of cash from your bank and handed it over to an unknown person. It took us until tonight to find the person."

I grinned despite myself.

Kenwood glanced towards the door, as though he thought he could escape. Jacobs wasn't looking panicked yet.

"And you found your answers?" I said at last.

"Yes. And I know you have kept this quiet, but with your permission, I'd like to clear that one up as well."

I nodded. It wasn't like Kenwood and Jacobs were going to report it, after all. And the others here would keep this quiet.

"Every year, Mr. Summerfield gives a large amount of money to a man working for the utility company, who uses it to pay the bills of people who are experiencing difficulties and to make certain they have heat, water, and electricity through the winter."

"Yeah, I bet. That your do-good little job, Sunflower? Trying to make yourself look good for the community --"

"That would only work if the community knew," Mr. Newspaperman said. He looked back at me. "The paper will not be reporting this."

"Thank you. The plan works best if I have others seek out those in need. I don't want to start getting overrun by scam artists."

"So, are we cleared up on all the trouble?" I asked. "I would like to get back to my apartment and rest."

"Almost," Krig said and looked almost apologetic for keeping me. "We were not only watching this apartment and everything Summerfield did, of course. With the supposed ties to the drug rings, we were keeping a closer watch on suspects in that field. And just an hour before the attack here, what do you think we saw, Mr. Kenwood and Mr. Jacobs?"

Neither spoke, but I could see the panic starting to ease up into Jacobs. Kenwood was just getting angrier.

"What is this bullshit?" he finally demanded. "You saw us talking to people? So what? It's our job. We are trying to uncover something that maybe others aren't so interested in as long as the payback is good enough --"

I really hadn't thought Kenwood was *that* stupid. Even Jacobs looked at him in shock. Krig lifted his hand; the police came over and handcuffed them both.

"What the hell --"

"You really don't want to say any more, Mr. Kenwood," Krig said. "These fine officers will read you your rights. Then all of us will be heading for the police station where we can have a nice long talk about your involvement with drug dealers and how you provoked an incident that only by pure luck got no one killed."

"You can't prove --"

"Oh, and I'll take the tape recorder too," he said and walked over to withdraw it out of Kenwood's pocket.

"That's my property --"

"And you will get it back," Krig said. "I think there might be things here we want to hear."

Kenwood went so pale one of the cops had to hold him to his feet.

Did he have recordings of the discussions with drug lords? Oh, now there might be something interesting. If I had felt even slightly better, I would have suggested that Tessa and I go with them to hear all of this. Instead, I watched them take the two back out, Kenwood cursing and Jacobs pale with fright.

Krig turned the recorder off. "I doubt we can get anything on them," Krig admitted. "But that doesn't mean we aren't going to spend some time looking and hold them while we do."

"Thank you." It was good enough right now.

Mr. Newspaperman gave me a more worried nod. "We will be printing a retraction, on the front page. Please let your sisters know. And we will not be printing anything more from Kenwood or Jacobs. We don't know how this report made it all the way to the front page without being authorized by anyone higher up. We will find out."

I knew how it happened -- magic. I couldn't tell him, though. If they decided to blame someone, we would have to set it right, but I only gave the man a nod and he hurried out. The councilman, without saying anything at all, followed.

Krig was the last one remaining behind with Tessa and me. He looked around the room as though he still expected to find something out of place.

He finally looked back at me. "We both know that there is something odd going on here with you and your people," he said. He lifted a hand before I could protest. "It's not drugs, it's not weapons -- and if it is a cult, it is the most beneficial one I've ever seen. I'm convinced this case is over. Someone higher up in the FBI may decide that you still are worth watching. Keep that in mind the next time you go and grab a lot of money out of an account and hand it over to someone under clandestine circumstances."

"I'll keep it in mind," I agreed.

He nodded and headed out.

"Well." Tessa said. He sat back in the chair and frowned. "That went better than we could have hoped."

I agreed and didn't move to get up just yet. "They won't be able to charge Jacobs and Kenwood with anything. We'll have to deal with the two of them again, but it's going to be without the weight of the newspaper behind them. And they're going to be worried about the FBI and the local police, I think."

"Yes," he agreed. "That's good. Can you get your sisters to pull back?"

"Not yet. They'll run with this for a while longer, but as soon as the newspaper prints the retraction, they'll be mollified for a while. I would not want to be Kenwood and Jacobs, though, because they will not forget those names."

Tessa smiled. He tapped my leg, and the pain disappeared again. "Let's get up to the apartment and spread the good news. That's two down."

"And only Dagan left," I said.

"He's not going to be so easy to handle."

I agreed with a sigh and we took the elevator up. I wanted to ask about what it meant to truly be Lord Summerfield, and not just a convenience we had used to get out of some trouble. I didn't. After the holidays, I told myself. Sometime before the new year. Yeah, I had a resolution now: learn what it means to be a Lord of the Fae.

My people were pleased to see me. They were having the kind of post work party where everyone just sprawled and looked pleased with the world. I took a chair at the table and Kala gave me cookies and tea.

"We survived it," I said aloud.

People laughed.

Tessa told them how the Kenwood/Jacobs/FBI fiasco had gone, which brought even more relief and celebration.

"We are still going to have trouble," I warned. "There are still paranoid, megalomaniac drug lords out there who aren't going to believe I haven't paid off everyone and I'm planning to take over their turf. We need to be careful."

The others nodded. I thought we might work a little magic to lessen the problem, too. Carefully. I was not going to turn into a vigilante.

I didn't, really, know what I would do next. We'd been working so hard to get from one point to the next that I hadn't looked on to the future.

"Summerfield?" Tessa said, sitting down by me.

"I am trying to think about what we need to do."

"Rest," Tessa said. Others agreed with weary nods. "Rest for now. We all need it."

"We have the Christmas Party here at The Fortress. Tomorrow, right?" I said.

"Yes," Tessa agreed. "I know; bouncing around in different times and places was getting a bit confusing."

"Our last problem is Dagan." I hated to say the name aloud for fear that I might call him. I held my breath. No lightning. No wind. "I am going to do some study, but to be honest, no one really knows enough about the Ancient Gods to give us a good answer."

"What should the rest of us do?" Kala asked.

"Let me handle Dagan as long as he doesn't drag me off again. He's part of the human world. For the rest, I am going to need instructions. I need to know what other fae will expect from me now. Before this, I really was just Lord Summerfield in name, you know. I never expected to have to deal with the others as well."

"True," Brandis agreed. "We'll start working up the list of things you need to learn."

I thought everything sounded calm. Relaxing. My leg still didn't hurt thanks to Tessa. We were going to have a nice gathering tonight --

My phone rang. Rose.

I gave a sigh and a wave for the others to be quiet.

"Hello Rose."

"We're on our way, Sunflower," she said. Her voice sounded subdued. "We need to talk. We'll be there in about five minutes. Just wanted to make certain you were around."

The phone went dead.

I dropped the cell phone on the table. "So much for the peace and quiet. My sister is on her way. I think maybe more than one of them. With luck, they won't be here for long."

I tried not to worry. Rose had sounded troubled, though. I didn't know what new misfortune had popped up now and that bothered me.

"Stay, Tessa," I said. "I can't be certain they haven't stumbled across something dealing with the fae. I might need you."

He looked bothered by the idea, but he got tea going and brought another plate of cookies -- I had the feeling we had leftovers from the Winter Court.

My sisters arrived. All five of them. We moved to the living room where they took the sofa and chairs, while I pulled over a chair and Tessa went into the kitchen, saying he was heading out in a few minutes.

Rose leaned forward. "We're worried, Sunflower. We're worried about mom."

"What's wrong?" I asked, panic rising.

"We think -- we think there's something she's not telling us. They showed up here without warning --"

"They've done that often enough before," I replied but still felt a wave of distress.

Rose nodded. "But today ... today mom took all of us *shopping*. We spent the entire day at the mall. She's *never* gone shopping with us before. Not mom. I fear --"

I was taking deep breaths. Long deep breaths -- but I couldn't hold back.

I started laughing. I couldn't stop and lifted a hand when

Rose went from startled to a narrow-eyed look that was going to get me in a lot of trouble.

"Sorry, sorry --" I wiped tears from my eyes. "That was -- was my fault."

"Your fault?"

"I asked her to keep you busy for a while so -- so I could have some peace. Said to make it a study of a different culture. I think -- I think she must have really gotten into the study."

They all stared at me.

And then Rose laughed. "Don't ever -- don't ever --"

"There will never be a chance like this again," I said, brushing tears from my face. Tessa gave a wave of his hand and headed out. "I'm sorry. But if you five had started badgering me on top of everything else -- Oh, you missed the FBI who came by with the police, someone from the paper, a city councilman and Kenwood and Jacobs. Kenwood and Jacobs left in handcuffs."

"Did they? Well, that's a good first step."

"The newspaper is working on finding out how the report made it to the front page without any high-end oversight. And yes, I think someone slipped it through somehow. The people running the newspaper are not stupid."

"I know. It's bothered me," Aster admitted.

"You're going to want us not to pursue suing the paper, aren't you?" Rose said with an exaggerated sigh.

"We'll see how contrite they are in the apology I get on the front page."

"The harm is done, though, Sunflower," Violet added with a shake of her head. "People are still going to believe."

"I know. But no amount of money is going to buy that

back. Besides, it turns out that Jacobs and Kenwood went straight to the drug lords with the tale, and that's what got them looking in my direction. So, here's the trade off, Rose: You guys get to have a go at the two of them. If they look like blithering idiots at the end, all the better."

"Finally -- someone pushed you far enough that you let us have some fun at it. Good. We'll start working up all the plan of attack."

"Thanks. I want them to think twice before they make trouble for me again. Oh, and if you happen across anything that says they're in contact with some guy named Gryn, let me know, okay? I can't say he's a problem, but I've started hearing his name, too."

"We will." Rose stood first, the other four -- as usual -- followed. "You get some rest. Are you okay?"

"Doing well. Had a nice, restful day," I said.

Rose laughed. They were all in a good mood as they left the building. I sat back and relaxed again. The apartment was empty. I couldn't remember the last time I'd been alone, except for the pixies. Even they were calm today, though, and they had curled up under the decorated tree in the corner, visible again now that my sisters were gone. They looked like a pile of green puppies who had played too hard. It was nice. Quiet.

I took advantage of the time to grab a couple books off the shelf and sit down to do a little research on our last problem. Dagan wasn't something my sisters could handle, though I think they would have given him a run for it. He was not of this world. He didn't understand the power that worked here.

I didn't have the power to stop him. I would have to find a way to divert him instead.

Later, I went out to the balcony and stared at the city. The day was cloudless, the sunlight bright. I would have been very cold, except the shield was up and no one could see me here right now. I stood there and drank in the feel of this place. My place. No matter what else had happened, this was here I belonged, and I thought maybe that was something I had been losing lately.

This is me. Penthouse apartment. Working for Woo Woo News.

No word from Glynis. Maybe after the newspaper wrote the retraction. Maybe....

I stared for a long time. Then I went in, showered, and went to bed again, just because I could. No Winter Court to go to. No Solstice Eve gathering or family party. All we had was the gathering here of friends tonight. Our own little group.

I slept well.

CHAPTER 22

I awoke to a major blizzard of the kind that made people huddle inside their homes and watch the snow build up from street to car bumper, to car door -- and higher.

By the time I showered and looked out from the balcony, the snow was up to the hoods of the cars outside The Fortress.

"What the hell has gone wrong now?" I demanded, with a wave at the street below us while snow fell around the shield.

Brandis shook his head in dismay. "We think that this might be nature and nothing more. Tessa has gone out to prowl around and see if he can pick up anything else, but we think this is just one of those big storms that blow in. We watched a bit of the Weather Channel. They were expecting it."

"Weather Channel. Good." I settled at the table. "No one is going anywhere today. Are we set? Is there anything we have to do?"

"Nothing," Brandis said. He looked at me, shaking his head. "You know that we really didn't think we'd pull this off, right?"

"I had that feeling, but here we are. What next?"

"A day of rest," Brandis said. "Rest and get ready for a

nice quiet fun night here at The Fortress. We're going to have trouble enough --"

A cold wind blew past us.

"Son of a bitch," Brandis mumbled.

Dagan appeared.

I gave him such a casual nod that it startled Brandis and somewhat unsettled our guest.

"I thought you might be here soon," I said. "We do have matters to discuss. Would you like some tea?"

I thought Brandis might hyperventilate. Tessa, Kala, and York all rushed through the door into the apartment, but I waved them to be calm.

Dagan watched me with a narrow-eyed stare that could mean anything. I didn't back down.

"Tea?" I said again.

He gave a nod. I waved to the table. He settled across from me while my people looked on, incredulous at the scene.

Tessa got the tea. He plainly didn't know what was going on, but it saved me from having to play servant, which was critical at this point. Tessa might not have realized it, but this worked in my favor.

I had thought about the problem last night. I had planned to talk to the others, but Dagan showed up too soon. No matter. I was willing to play this one out on my own.

We sipped tea. I sat my cup down and faced Dagan. "We have a problem. You have been hanging around enough by now to know things have changed dramatically from when you were last present on earth."

"This does not make me any less powerful."

"I know. The question is really what you want to do with

that power."

"I do not intend to share it."

I gave a wave of my hand. "You already are sharing it and not just with me. You know that there are so many gods and powers in the world now that you are far from the most powerful. I don't intend to pursue more power, though. I am what I am, for whatever that might be."

"And?"

"And the area where you should be the most powerful is in sad need of someone to help straighten things out. Maybe, rather than pursuing someone who really isn't interested in your power or your place, you might turn your attention there for a while."

"While you gain the power to defeat me."

"I do not need to defeat you. I do not want your place or your power. I want to help my own people. I want peace. What is it you really want, Dagan?"

His eyes narrowed again. The wind blew -- he was not happy. I needed to offer him something more.

"I give you my word that I mean you no harm and that I am not interested in your power or your place. My actions have brought you back into the world, though, and by that you are my responsibility. I do not want to see harm come to anyone for it."

He blinked. I think he saw the problem and one that I didn't want to say aloud just now.

I had brought him back into the world. I had power over him because of that tie. I was willing to help him to do well in the world.

He sipped his tea.

My people still looked panicked. They knew I didn't have the magical power to use against him. I don't think they understood the world of humans, though. Dagan, for all his power, was part of my world, not theirs.

We sipped more tea.

"I have trouble understanding this world," Dagan finally admitted.

A breakthrough. An admission that Dagan was out of his depth. I did not leap in and tell him I had all the answers.

"This part of the world is far from where you ruled," I explained. "Far in time and culture. However, I have sat by the fires of tribes still roaming your desert lands and the mountains of the Hindu Kush. I have talked with people who were as lost in this modern world as you are."

"And you think I should go to them and that they will follow me?"

"No, they won't follow you. But I believe you can help those people anyway."

He sat back. "And why would I?"

"Because you need purpose and a better link to this world than me. This isn't your place. You can never be more than you are now if you stay here and keep following me. I know why you haven't destroyed me. I know you can, but if you do, then you lose your link back to this world again. What you want is for me to accept you as the Lord of the World. It's not going to happen. If you do not find a different cause and link, you're going to be following me around like a puppy."

"You have followers. You put them in danger and at my mercy."

"And you could find that I am far less reasonable if my

people are in danger. Do you want me to investigate how I might trap you back in your temple? Shall I start studying the Elamites?"

He sat back this time, startled.

"I have access to knowledge, and I have the people to find more," I warned. I sipped tea again, giving him a moment to calm. "This is your chance to make your own way in the world. You can help the world, because if you don't, and if you bother me, then we'll be having this conversation again. I don't think you will like my final decision in that case."

He looked across at me, eyes narrowed still. I sipped my tea. He sipped his.

He put his cup down, gave a barely perceptible nod, and disappeared.

I took another sip of tea.

"I think you're crazy," Tessa said, throwing himself into the chair where Dagan had been a moment before. "When did you go stark raving mad?"

"About the time the first troll tried to kill me," I replied. I put down the cup. "I think that worked, but we'll have to keep an eye on the area. I don't want him doing things to make matters worse."

"Elamites?" Brandis asked.

I smiled brightly. "In the ancient world, the Elamites were a people feared for their magic."

"Ah," Tessa said. "Yes. You could have told us."

"I didn't have time, and we needed to get Dagan settled." I looked out into the snowy weather. Ice hung from my balcony, a sign of the warmth where Dagan had passed. "I hoped he wouldn't drop in on the gathering. Last night, when things finally started calming down, I had a chance to think through the situation. He's had the power to kill me, you know. But he didn't. I figured out why."

"I seriously doubt this is over," Brandis said. He settled at the table too. "A being of that power isn't going to go quietly away and do your bidding."

"I know. So, we'll be doing some Elamite studies. However, right now, we have a chance for one night without a major holiday fiasco. I don't think that's too much to ask for after everything else."

"Don't tempt fate," Tessa mumbled.

"I've had some people out keeping an eye on the drug lords," Brandis said. He waved a hand before I could say anything. "That's my job, and we needed to know if there were any problems brewing in that direction. They appeared to be working themselves up into a new frenzy --"

"Damn."

"-- but they ran into some unexpected difficulties. Car problems for a couple. A rather annoying police raid at the entirely wrong time for another. We aren't going to do anything obvious, Summerfield. However, we will do our best to make certain they don't cause trouble for you, and with luck, none for others as well."

This had to be a matter of trust. Even though they were not from this realm, I believed my friends would do their best not to create trouble that would change the world in ways none of us wanted.

"I think --" I started at stopped. The others turned to look my way, and I could see an anxious eagerness in their faces. These were people who wanted to do good. "I think if we are very careful, we might make things better for more than people here in The Fortress."

"As you have already been doing," Tessa said. "We follow your lead, you know. Your work, attitude, and commitment are what sets our tone."

"And if I decided to take over the world and enslave everyone with magic?"

"We'd be looking for the real Summerfield," Brandis said. "We have chosen to stay with you for a reason. We don't follow blindly. We follow where we think the person is deserving. Even a clan leader can be replaced, you know."

"I don't know. I need to learn *everything*."

"Give us a little time," Tessa replied. "Until the first of the year. We need to think about all the things we know that seem natural to us and we might not think to tell you."

"And what things I shouldn't know," I added.

Tessa and Brandis both looked startled by that idea. Brandis was the one who shook his head first.

"There is nothing we won't tell you," he said and leaned closer. "You are now a part of our world, Lord Sunflower Breeze Summerfield. There will be no secrets between us."

Trust. I hoped I lived up to their expectations.

CHAPTER 23

The day before Christmas turned out to be as calm as things went in my life. My parents stopped by despite the storm. I had the joy of telling my mother how badly the girls had taken to going shopping with her.

"Is that what was wrong?" She laughed with delight. "These women are impossible to please, you know!"

"Oh, I know," I said emphatically.

Dad, who had never known quite what to do with his bevy of daughters, just gave a nod of agreement.

"We're heading off for the hinterlands of Nepal tomorrow," Mom said. She leaned over and put a hand on my arm. "You have got to start taking care, Sunflower. I don't think things are going to be any safer for you."

"No safer," I agreed. "But I'll do my best to stay safe. You two take care as well."

"We will," Dad said. He looked around the apartment as though he only now noticed it. "Can't believe you ended up living in a place like this, SB. Don't you miss the wide-open spaces?"

"All the time," I admitted with a glance toward the balcony and the world outside. "But you know, you can get used to not being rained on and having hot water from a faucet. And pizza."

They both laughed, but I could tell they were not going to envy me.

We visited for a while, and they said not to come to see them off. My parents had always hated emotional goodbyes at airports. I hugged them both and thought about going off with them.

My friends and I had eggnog and watched *A Christmas Story*, which seemed to transcend the human/fae line of humor. They laughed as much as I did.

I napped again, trying to catch up on all the missed sleep. I awoke to a perfect Christmas Eve, with a light snow and the smell of rolls baking. I came out to find Tessa and Kala in the kitchen, apparently baking the old-fashioned way.

"What are you two doing?" I asked with a laugh.

"Learning the ways of the human," Kala replied and sounded somber. "We're learning what it is like to really be a part of this world. It's part of the education we need to show you our ways."

"And?"

"You people work very hard, even for the little joyful things," Kala said, surprising me. "And if you work this hard for something fun, how much harder to work to get food, warmth, and clothing?"

"And you don't have to work at all?" I asked.

"Not in the same way. We have limits," Tessa said. "And we have our focus directed in other ways. We often focus on art, for instance, which can't simply be wished into existence. We also have to work in cooperation because magic would be wasted otherwise."

"Which is why you have clans," I said.

"That and protection, though not so often from other clans like it has been lately. There are other dangers," Tessa said. He grinned suddenly. "Trolls and such."

"Not what we want to discuss today," Kala said. She drew cinnamon rolls from the oven. "Hey. I think these turned out!"

We had hot rolls, sharing with the others who wandered by. The newspaper arrived, severely delayed by the weather.

And there, on the front page, was what I had hoped to see:

FBI Clears Summerfield of all charges.

I scanned the report which said Kenwood and Jacobs had concocted the story as a scam, were now under arrest for inciting the shooting incident.

Kenwood, despite the words of caution from his lawyer, told the reporter that the only way Sunflower Breeze Summerfield could have gotten out of this trouble was with enough money.

Mr. Kenwood was now looking for a new lawyer.

And below that was a lengthy apology note from the newspaper itself for having been duped into this mess by someone who had on occasion written for them, but who would not be doing so again.

"Well," I said with a smile. "That certainly helps brighten the day. Let's go party."

I went downstairs, using the elevator and the cane and silently cursing some people, weapons, and wondering if I could dare *wish* for something to happen to them right then.

We had eight children in the building. They were already there and making enough noise for twice as many -- but it was happy noise. They each had new toys. The little girls were ecstatic about the castle and the three boys less so until they found out they all had armor and play swords.

I had not expected the Queen of the Fae to arrive, and the surge of magic back by the stairs startled us all. She came dressed in gold and silver woven into a flowing gown that glittered as she moved. I'd forgotten she said she would be here. I realized that the fae giving their word was something binding and they would expect the same from me. Since I had never purposely gone back on my word, this wasn't a big problem. Still, it helped me to understand them better.

At least she hadn't just popped in, which would have been hard to explain.

There was more to her being here than just a promise. She seemed to adore the children who thronged around her in her fancy dress as she sat down to tell them stories.

We had quiet then.

"Tessa, can you go back to the apartment and get that paperwork Rose brought?"

He gave a quick nod and darted off, smiling. The parents had gathered off to a side table, content as they watched the children. I was about to make them all a little happier with the world.

I hobbled over, and they made a place for me.

"I have something for the rest of you -- no, don't say anything. Tessa will be here in a moment."

They looked bothered, but I smiled, and we listened to the story the Winter Queen told until Tessa showed up.

My cell phone chimed. Text? I didn't get text very often.

Merry Christmas SB. We'll get things worked out. Glynis.

I smiled, almost daring to wish she were here. But not yet. I still had more drug lord problems to clear up. I simply texted back *Thank you. Happy Holidays. Be well.*

Tessa came back with a briefcase. I took out the papers and passed them around to the others.

"What is this?" Pam asked.

"This is the paperwork for trust accounts for each of your children. By the time they are old enough, they will have the money for a good college education. If they do not go to college, they'll only get a part of the money and only when they are older. If they go to college, they get the tuition paid plus a hefty allowance while they are there. And if something happens to any of you, or to me for that matter, they will have money to care for them."

Silence. Eyes stared my way.

"Summerfield --" Pam began.

"It's done. You can't undo it. The accounts are set up, and these are your copies of the work. My sisters will take care of all the particulars."

"Why?" Pablo asked.

"Because I can, and I believe in making a better world, one person at a time. All of you are going to help me do more in the future."

"Yes," Pam said. She held the papers tightly.

So that was done, too. I had obligations. Others might not see it as so, but I did. Just because my ties were now with the fae did not mean I was going to turn my back on the people around me.

A little later the Queen told another story and this time she sent up globes of colored light that broke apart and dropped snowflakes down on the children who ran around trying to catch them.

I reached up and caught one that came my way. It glowed in my hand.

"That's just incredible. How does she do that?" Pam said.

I smiled as I turned to Pam and held out the snowflake. "It's magic."

THE END

PREVIEW: SUMMERFIELD 4: SPRING BREAK

CHAPTER 1

I have a problem with the weather. Well, not a problem precisely created by me, but the trouble manifests where I am since I am linked to fae clans and an unhappy ancient god of storms.

The inclement -- not to say unnatural -- weather had started with a summer storm last year (dropping trolls in Omaha), went on to a massive autumn ice storm (which brought an unhappy fae prince), passed into winter blizzards (the Fae's Winter Court), and now lurked nearby as we headed back to warmer days. I often watched the sky and hoped for the best.

Like that had worked so far.

Spring had arrived in Omaha, though, and welcome for the 'at least it's above freezing' warmth and not as many storms as we'd had during the winter. My fae friends were learning to temper their magical outbursts, which had been part of the trouble. They also monitored anything Dagon, the Assyrian God of Storms, tossed our way. He tested my resolve to remain in place as Summerfield, Lord of the Earth

Realm -- at least that was my title at the fae court. Unfortunately, that title and the power had unsettled the ancient God.

In what used to pass for my 'real' life, I was also the chief reporter for Wolton World News -- or Woo Woo News, as we all called it these days. We were the world's top paranormal newspaper, which is saying something. Julia, my boss, remains adamant that our reports stay factual. Even around Omaha, enough odd happenings were going on -- and not all of them associated with the Fae -- to keep us busy.

This was a Saturday, and I had two significant events on my agenda for the day. As things went for a Fae Lord, this didn't look so bad. Except that those events were ... well, troubling.

The first was an invitation to tea with the Fae Queen.

The second was dinner with my five sisters.

I wasn't certain which of them worried me more.

I hadn't seen the Queen of the Fae since the Winter Solstice gathering that I'd hosted. That had been an unsettling little occasion, which included several assassination attempts. I had taken wounds -- but they had been trying to kill her. Not a good way to start my official role as a Fae Lord, never mind one who wasn't Fae.

I didn't know why she asked me to tea today. I was nervous, and my fae companions had become unsettled since the summons. Even Brandis, the Dragon Clan's Warlord, looked uneasy. Tessa had started pacing. He would be my companion since the invitation made a point of saying Tessa should be my single guard.

Why was I being called to the meeting? I would meet her

on the borderlands between Fae and human realms. I had yet to go to the fae lands themselves, and I didn't mind since I had more enemies there than I liked to consider.

Tessa and I dressed for the occasion in my official colors of green fields, blue skies, and golden flowers worked into a subtle array. Tessa looked good. I hoped to pull it off half as well.

We could walk into any sort of trouble. I wanted to leave Tessa behind, but I couldn't tell him to remain since she had invited him. Besides, Tessa was my usual guard. He'd wandered into many problems with me in the past, and we knew how each other reacted.

I thought he looked less nervous now that we were ready to go. I tried to copy that attitude. Then I saw him blink and his eyes go unfocused. I wasn't the only one who stopped and waited, hoping the Cat Clan Totem had a vision that would help me navigate the meeting.

A moment later, he took a breath and shook his head. "I don't know," he admitted. "I just see nothing definite, and what I do sense seems more here than there. Here in the human world, I mean."

I looked around at my other companions. Cat Clan, Dragon Clan, and Centaur Clan members had all gathered in my apartment to see me off. I felt like I was about to step aboard the Titanic.

They worried about me as much as I worried about them. Tessa and I started for the door -- but then I stopped and turned back to them. They all looked my way. I was about to say something they would not like. I braced myself because it was not easy for me, either.

"Do whatever you need to do to survive," I told them. The group started to protest. "I know, I know. This doesn't have to be something wrong. I wish we knew -- but I still want you to be careful. If Queen Amata has decided that she's not happy with me after all, then you should be ready for the change. I also have real enemies, you know. Some people might take advantage of Tessa and I being gone, no matter what is going on with the Queen."

"That's true," Kala agreed. She glanced out the balcony windows toward the sky. Dagon plagued us with storms at a whim. I kept hoping he would stop focusing on me, but I made an easy target for his frustrations with the world's new ways. Reasoning with Dagon was not possible. I didn't know what we might try next.

"Don't forget about human enemies. There are still drug lords who think I'm going to take over their territories. There are also Jacobs and Kenwood. They've had enough time to get some courage back and to come up with another stupid plan to cause me trouble. Pam's divorce goes to the judge in less than two months. He has to realize that his past actions will not count in his favor."

"So, he'll do something more?" Asta, a member of the Centaur Clan, asked. She'd started feeling comfortable hanging around with the Cat Clan and Dragon Clan people who were my usual companions.

"Oh yes," Tessa said with a disgusted nod. "If there were ever two humans stupid enough to try something again, it will be them. They'll think Summerfield is here, and since you can't tell them where he is or produce him, they'll assume you are lying. That alone could set them off."

Asta blinked several times. She hadn't dealt with humans for long, unlike the Cat Clan people who had remained trapped here for centuries.

"Oh, and don't forget Gryn," Kala added with a special snarl directed at her former Warlord. "He might know about Summerfield's invitation and think we'll be easier to take without our Lord in residence. He'll be wrong, of course."

"Dagon won't strike if Summerfield isn't here," Tessa added. He looked at the sky. "Worry more about Gryn and whoever is working with him. Just keep safe."

Nods.

I started for the door again. Then I stopped and turned back, winning a frustrated sigh from Tessa and a few smiles around the room.

I did something I had refrained from in most cases. "I am Lord Summerfield," I said aloud. Tessa gave me a worried glance. He knew I didn't throw that title out there on a whim. "And I order you, as your Lord, to do everything you can to keep yourselves safe if you need to."

"Summerfield." Tessa sighed with frustration.

"Should I have not said so?" I asked, looking at him.

His eyes went odd once more. He seldom got visions, and two in such short order meant all kinds of trouble. He looked at me and shook his head. "Maybe it was wise to say. And I know you don't have to tell the others to look after you."

That sounded like I would soon have trouble. Or maybe not. We'd had a few odd attacks over the last months of winter. Spring had come, and things seemed better. Maybe Tessa just thought about the danger he might walk into with me.

"Tessa --"

"We don't want to be late," he said and urged me toward the door and all the way out into the hall before I could think to say more.

We were running behind time. So much so that Tessa herded me to the elevator instead of the stairs. Gremlins had followed us that far -- little green creatures who were invisible to everyone but the Fae and me. I sent them back to the apartment before they caused trouble.

Kala and Brandis followed us, and I did not order them back. We had no trouble heading through the building and to the children's castle we'd built inside the former garage. It was a nice safe place for the kids who lived in the apartment building, and it held a secret for my people. Behind the back wall stood a magical doorway to other places.

There were dangers associated with that portal placed in human lands, but a necessary tool for my people. We'd had too much trouble of late, and even I'd felt that something worse waited on the horizon. Tessa's visions, which he couldn't quite decipher, didn't help. What if going to the Queen was a bad idea?

No choice.

Brandis took down the magic that kept the portal hidden on our side. He still didn't look any happier about our journey.

"One more thing," I said. All three of my fae companions straightened, and I could see rebellion in their faces. I lifted a hand for calm. "Just remember that I have dinner with my sisters tonight. If I am running late, do whatever you can to keep them placated. I'll do everything I in my power to make sure that I do not miss that gathering."

Oh, they believed I wouldn't miss that one. Why had the Queen and the Unholy Five decided they all had to see me on the same day? What kind of game was Karma playing with me this time? I'd done little out of the ordinary, even for a human, let alone a fae lord, since the Winter Court. We all wanted quiet.

Tessa looked at me. I nodded. Brandis and Kala moved up closer in case anything leapt through. We'd had trouble in the portal before, so this wasn't just unwarranted paranoia on our side. By rights, we should have closed it down. However, the gateway provided easy access out of The Fortress -- what we called the apartment block -- to reach other places. Some of my Fae had used it to visit home. The Cat Clan had stayed trapped in the human world for centuries, and they still did not have their Key back, which was in the hands of a treacherous former warlord for the Clan. Gryn remained out of sight.

Using the portal might pull him out of hiding.

The tunnel beyond glowed brightly with white light and looked as smooth as glass. The walls curved upward in a semicircle that shimmered and shifted -- not good when you were trying to see if anything moved out there that shouldn't be.

We spotted something. We all stepped back, hands moving -- but I recognized two of the Queen's own guards. I gave a little sigh of relief. Better them rather than some monster.

"We will escort you through," the man in the lead said.

"Thank you," I replied with a blow of my head, and I tried

not to think they had arrived to make sure I didn't back out of the meeting.

I knew my paranoia about having tea with the Fae Queen had become unreasonable. I fought it back and gave a pleasant nod to Brandis and Kala. Tessa and I stepped forward. We had one guard in front of us and the other behind -- and yes, I felt safer for it.

The tunnel, though, took longer to traverse than it had to the Winter Palace. I glanced at Tessa with a slight frown. "This is taking longer."

"Queen Amata has provided this link, Summerfield. The distance is farther from the Fortress to the Borderlands than it is to travel within the human realm."

"I suppose so," I replied and straightened my sleeve -- a nervous gesture, but it kept my hands busy. "There are still far too many things that I need to know."

He gave a brief nod and said no more. This wasn't a good time for a new 'teaching Lord Summerfield the basics' lesson.

I had never been to the borderlands or to the fae lands. I had held even the Winter Solstice gathering in the human realm, where my hodgepodge of a clan had built a stunning ice castle for the event. If some fae just had stopped trying to assassinate me during the celebration --

Well, some humans had tried to kill me, too, and come damned close.

I am paranoid these days, and there are reasons why my fae followers don't like to let me out of their sight. Tessa was so twitchy right now that I feared he would go cat at any moment. The shape-changing Cat Clan totem had become my most common companion, and as a result, also the most paranoid.

The guards gave nothing away, though they had their hands on their belted swords. I didn't take that as anything more than a natural reaction to being around me since I drew trouble.

We neared the end of the portal. It felt more ... alive, I guess. The scent of flowers filled the air, and I heard the faint ripple of running water. I relaxed, though I saw Tessa pulling at his sleeves and even pushing his unruly hair back. We were about to meet with Queen Amata, and he might be almost as worried as me. We both knew that she could order the Cat Clan totem to return to the fae lands and disassociate himself from me. His Clan had gone hundreds of years without their totem.

However, she could have made that order without inviting me to tea.

We stepped into ... somewhere else. This was not the human realm, though I could still sense some of my world in the makeup. I also felt the soft tingle of magic in the air that came from the fae lands.

A slight mist gave way to a beautiful glade. I took a deep breath of the sweet air. Birds of blue and green darted through the flowering trees nearby, and multi-colored butterflies drifted across the low-lying plants. A path of white stone led through dozens of flowers all the way to a table and two chairs. The Queen, dressed in an elegant floor-length dress of white and pink, sat in one chair. She beaconed me forward. Behind her, a small waterfall cast rainbows where the light touched it.

I nodded to Tessa. He knew the rules and that I had to

go on alone now. Tessa moved off with the two guards. I always relied on Tessa to steer me out of trouble with fae customs. Going to sit with the Queen without him to nudge me -- I panicked again.

I didn't know enough about fae culture to face something like this with any sort of assurance. My people had been trying to teach me, but we'd had little time between one disaster and the next. I knew how to waltz with the Queen of the Fae, but that wouldn't help much today.

So, I concentrated and forced calm into my mind again as I walked toward the Queen. I didn't spend enough time in nature anymore, and I couldn't even blame the Fae for that, either. They'd much rather be out in the wilds than in the city -- well, at least if they could still get pizza delivery.

That thought brought my sense of humor back. By the time I reached the table and gave a proper bow, I felt better. I worried about why the Queen wanted to see me, but I didn't think it was something too dire if we were meeting in a place like this.

"Please join me, Lord Summerfield," she said with a wave to the wicker chair across from hers. She smiled. Better still.

"Thank you." Using my title gave me a little more confidence.

One of her guards brought over a tray and placed it on the table. It held a teapot filled with a vanilla-scented liquid and a plate of petit fours along with small plates and cups for the two of us.

I forced calm and steadied my hands. "Shall I pour?" I asked with a nod to the tea.

"Yes, thank you."

That seemed a show of trust, too. Still hovering nearby, the guard gave me a slight frown of worry, but he left at the Queen's signal. I poured for both of us. She waved a bejeweled hand to the petit fours, and I placed one on my plate. She took two and smiled like a child stealing an extra sweet.

It was a pleasant smile. I calmed more again.

"Queen Amata," I said at last. I held the cup in my hand but had not sipped. "If I have done anything wrong --"

"You have not," she replied and then tilted her head. "I am sorry if I gave you that impression. Be at ease, Lord Summerfield. I asked you to tea, not to your removal from power. Tessa --"

She stopped as she glanced at Tessa over with the Fae guards. I thought she maybe had not looked at him too closely until now, and I wasn't sure if that was a good thing or not.

"I fear he's spent too much time in the human realm," I stated in her silence. She gave me a measured look, the slightest hint of a frown. "I've offered to let them all return. Many times. I'm sorry --"

"They are all where they need to be," she replied.

How could I argue with such a pronouncement? I had considered asking her to call them all home, and out of the danger they faced with me, but I was glad when she said those words. I still didn't know why I was here, though.

She sipped her tea and ate one of the small cakes, and so did I. She put down her cup. I held tighter to mine, despite believing that I wasn't in danger from her.

She had still called me here for a reason.

"I have asked you to tea because I am worried for you, not about you. I am not sure how I can help you with this problem, either. You seem to have some trouble with the weather."

"Ah. Dagon," I said with a nod and what came as a strange relief, given that Dagon was an old God. "I am trying to work out the problem with him. He thinks I have encroached on his powers by taking up the Earth's rule as a Fae Lord. Most of what he throws my way is annoying but not dangerous as long as we can dampen the winds and control any chance of flooding. I'm uncertain how to deal with him."

"He is one of the most ancient deities. There are others, many others, who might have made the same claim against you as well, though. Why has he?"

"We have a special link. When I was much younger, I fell into his temple and drew his attention after a long, long sleep."

"I had a vision that he will cause you some additional difficulty. The trouble involves storms, of course -- but I could not see more. It is not a matter for the fae realm, and my prescience in your world is limited."

"I appreciate the warning," I said with another bow of my head. More trouble from Dagon. Great. "Do you have any suggestions?"

She smiled and, this time, fiercer. "There have been times when Fae brought an Elder Power to face the Justice of the Fae Court. Unfortunately, the Old Court is still a duel to the death between the deity and the one who brought him up on charges. I don't suggest it."

"Dagon and I fight to the death? If that were the only

option, I might as well go stand on a mountain top and shout insults at him and throw myself off the peak, saving him the trouble."

"Ha. You would surprise Dagon, at least. But no, I don't suggest such strategies, even with your Fae at your back. You might consider the New Court, though."

"New Court?" I wished my Fae had thought to tell me these things.

"We have adapted and adopted ways from your world. All beings of our type -- Fae, human, even Elder Gods live by basic rules and many understandings. When they flaunt such conventions, they might be summoned to the New Court. We now have lawyers."

I looked at her with a nervous shake of my head, trying to get that chill away that had run down my back. "Fae lawyers? I have five sisters --"

"Yes," she said and I wasn't surprised to find out she knew about my family. "I wonder how they would do with such a case."

I must have looked as appalled as I felt. I shook my head in mute denial and then forced words to return as I banished the thought of my sisters involved with the Fae in any way.

"They drive me crazy," I offered as an excuse for my bad manners, and she nodded. "How do you handle fae lawyers?"

"Let us say that I do not invite them to tea."

We both laughed. "I am to have dinner with my sisters tonight," I admitted.

"I won't keep you."

"Oh, I don't mind being a little late."

She laughed again, and the birds sang a brighter song at

the sound. I had a wonderful tea with the Queen of the Fae. We discussed the others who were part of my small Clan, and she smiled at Vane's love of pizza, which had become somewhat infamous among her people.

"Vane is growing up," I said and hoped that I didn't sound too sad about it. The Dragon Clan needed their totem to be older and wiser. "I'm not sure he'll outgrow his love of pizza. We have curtailed his dragon form from eating technology, though."

She thought I had joked, but when she saw my face, Queen Amata laughed again. We talked of others, including the Centaur clan members who had taken an oath with me at a time of genuine danger.

"I have told them they are free to return to their own people," I said but shrugged. "I understand why they don't go. Roan and Gryn are still moving against me. I can't guess how much of Centaur Clan back them. It can't be safe for anyone who sided with me, and I'm glad to have their company."

"You realize they might work for Gryn, though."

"Yes, I thought it possible. The same could be true of many Cat Clan people since he was their Warlord. I will trust them all until I learn otherwise."

"And hope you survive it."

"That, too."

"I think you don't realize that a fae judges you, not only by your actions but also by the people you keep as followers, from Vane and Tessa all the way to Prince Arinith."

"I have been lucky in my friends," I said and glanced from her to Tessa. He still talked with the guards, and I wondered what information they passed back and forth.

"More than luck," she replied. "The Fae do not follow just for luck. You helped to stop a long war between the Cat and Dragon Clans. You are useful and ingenious. And I fear I must go back to my court now."

"Thank you for inviting me," I said and stood with a bow.

"It was a wonderful break from duties," Queen Amata admitted and rose as well. Then she stared into my face. "Beware of Dagon."

Surprise Short Story

Author Vs. Character

Outline and Notes
Chapter Five

Author: The night passes quietly. Character sleeps soundly and wakes up at first light. Rooster crows. Climbs down from the hay loft and stretches, pleased to see that the fog of the night before has cleared and he can now see the town -- a couple dozen buildings, including a travelers' inn. He'd found refuge in their stable. Grateful for the chance to sleep so comfortably --

Character: You know, I've been quiet and gone along with you for the previous four chapters without a complaint, but this is too much. I've spent six days sleeping on leaves, huddled by a tree in the rain, and half-drowned and miserable. And now you think sleeping in a hay pile is comfortable? I tossed and turned all night. Hay isn't down feathers, you know -- its dried *twigs*. They *stab*. And what the hell is this? *(Holds up something between his fingers.)*

Author: *(Peers closely)* Looks like a needle to me.

Character: Right. What perverted person would put a needle in a pile of hay? It jabbed me.

Author: Did it? *(Looks hopefully at the needle and then glances at research books)* Is it rusty? Tetanus . . . severe muscle spasms, also called lockjaw . . . this might be interesting! I hadn't thought of that sort of illness, before they had shots and everything. Let me see it.

Character: See what?

Author: The needle!

Character: *(Brushing hands)* What needle? There's no needle here . . . and no tetanus.

Author: *(Reluctantly puts aside the books)* Oh well. Okay, where were we?

Character: New day, no fog, etc.

Author: Right. Okay. Character makes his way through the stable yard and past the open door to the inn's kitchen --

Character: His stomach growling --

Author: If you're hungry, eat the journey bread in your pocket.

Character: Are you joking? That stuffs so hard I could chip rocks with it. A caveman with this journey bread could have ruled the world.

Author: Character walks past the door and out into the street where he sees something that makes him *shut up* and forget everything else. There, on the hilltop overlooking the village, is the black stone castle that has haunted his dreams for the last five years! He anxiously turns that way, heading toward the distant castle gate --

Character: Are you crazy? Or do you just think I'm stupid?

Author: What's the problem now? That's the castle -- your goal in sight --

Character: Yeah, *the castle*. Those dreams would be the ones where I wake up in a cold sweat, screaming because the castle sucked me in and buried me alive. And now you expect me to blithely head straight up and walk in? To hell with that. I'm heading the opposite way on this road, just as fast as I can --

Author: Back towards the toll gate and the guards you so carefully avoided last night? Oh, good plan.

Character: Damn. I forgot. What's to the right?

Author: A fetid swamp still curling with the last tendrils of the fog from the night before. It must once have been part of a lake and port. Character can even make out the masts of ships buried in the muck, vines twining up across tattered sails, as well as the bleached bones of men, trapped within those ropes of green, as though the plants had suddenly reached out and grabbed them --

Character: I get the idea. Thank you so much for another new level of nightmare to add to my others. What's to the left?

Author: To the east -- left for Characters not paying attention to where they are --can be seen a few more buildings, some of them obviously abandoned. Beyond that are rocky fields and small plots of dying plants. Less than a mile away is the shadow of the forest --

Character: Excellent! Oh, and may I say that five chapters is a bit too long to be waiting for a name?

Author: I want it to be the right name, the perfect name. I'll know it when I see it.

Character: Fine. Whatever. Character casts one worried look at the brooding black castle and sets off on foot past the falling buildings and into the fields --

Author: Almost immediately, Character hears the baying of dogs and looks worriedly toward the castle. He can see the pack that is pacing beneath the walls, possibly waiting for the morning meal. But now they've seen him moving in the empty land below --

Character: Shit.

Author: Don't worry. They're only poodles.

Character: A pack of poodles? Toy? Miniature? Standard?

Author: A mix. And actually, they're only half poodle.

Character: *(Eyeing them cautiously and trying to guess if he can reach the forest and get away from them)* Half poodle and half what?

Author: Wolf.

Character: *(Stops and shakes head)* Wolves. You crossed poodles and wolves. And the reason was...?

Author: Wild killers, less fur to clean up. They have spotted Character, and the woodle pooves bay -- or maybe yip -- again.

Character: Woodle pooves. I'm getting an image of the dogs here ... oh man, that's just *wrong*.

Author: Are you trying for the trees or not?

Character: Can I make it?

Author: Probably. They're kind of inbred woodle pooves. Not entirely bright.

Character: Okay then. Better than the castle.

Author: Character jogs along the broken path between the rocks as the woodle pooves gather at the top of the hill. He's more than halfway to the cursed forest before they --

Character: *(Stops)* Cursed forest? You didn't say anything about the forest being cursed!

Author: Let's see: Deadly swamp, dying fields, big brooding black castle . . . of course the forest is cursed. Duh.

Character: Good point. My mistake. What kind of curse?

Author: *(Flips through notes)* A century ago a major battle was fought at the village. A mage-king, seeing all about to be lost, cast a desperate spell to save his throne. He brought not only the plants of the lake but also the trees of the forest into the battle. They won, but unfortunately, the trees developed a taste for blood. They won't kill you . . . well, not right away. You can escape in a couple years. You won't be sane, of course, but I think you might be an interesting character if you were insane.

Character: I don't need a cursed forest of vampire trees to drive me crazy: I've got you. Character, sensing something evil from the forest -- or maybe not wanting to risk his luck with the woodle pooves -- turns around and hurries back to the village.

Author: Character soon reaches the street and turns toward the castle.

Character: No.

Author: What do you mean no? You've found out there is no other direction you can go. Now start up for the castle --

Character: I am not going to that frigging castle!

Author: Do you know how long I've been setting up this moment? That castle has been in your dreams --

Character: *Nightmares*

Author: -- for five years! You've been pursuing it since you came of age!

Character: I had dreams about Daisy from the *Bread and Barrel* for ten years! Why couldn't I pursue her instead?

Author: This isn't that kind of book!

Character: Like I haven't noticed!

Author: Character, reluctantly realizing he has no choice, and that this is his destiny, heads for --

Character: The privy. It has to be around here by the inn somewhere.

Author: You're just putting off the inevitable.

Character: Where is the privy? Or we're going to have something else inevitable happen.

Author: The privy is at the opposite side of the stable. Character can see the swarms of flies and flinches at the stench as he nears --

Character: Bullshit.

Author: I don't think bulls have anything to do with this problem.

Character: Look, this is stupid. The world has magic. The first thing they're going to use it for is to fix the stink from the outhouse! Character heads for the privy, noting the faint scent of lilacs and roses. Butterflies dance in the air.

Author: As he slips in and closes the door --

Character: A little privacy, if you don't mind. Out.

Author: . . .

Author: . . .

Author: . . .

Character: Character steps back out, looking towards the door to the kitchen again.

Author: Too bad you don't have any money.

Character: Character digs into jacket and pulls out a shiny silver coin.

Author: You've been holding out on me.

Character: I got it off one of those five bandits who tried to kill me back in Chapter Three. You know, right before the bridge -- the one that had borne the weight of a thousand peasants and their wagons -- gave way under me for no apparent reason and I nearly drowned.

Author: Yeah, but you lost the bandits who were trying to kill you.

Character: I'm going for breakfast. Then I'm going to lay low for the rest of the day and escape the way I got in. Don't even bother to say anything. *Character goes in and orders food, has a quiet leisurely meal, lingering over bread and honey. The local serving wench isn't bad looking, either. She reminds him of Daisy, the girl he left behind. They might have a pleasant day together. He finishes up the food, pushing away the plate --*

Author: And the guards, having been relieved of their posts at the gate, come in for their own breakfast. They immediately spot Character and know he's a stranger who didn't come through their gate. Worse, though, is that they recognize him.

Character: What? I've never been here! They can't --

Author: The guards fall on him and he's soon beaten to his knees --

Character: Beaten? But -- but --

Loter, Captain of the Guard: Another one! You look like your great-grandfather, boy! We're not going to have any more mad mage-kings here!

Selis, another guard: I didn't think that dream crap would work, but hell, what is this? Fifteen of them now? Up boy.

Author: Selis grabs Character by the arm and hoists him to his feet, taking him outside. Captain Loter loops a rope around his arms and ties it to his saddle --

Character: But --

Author: Loter kicks his horse into a trot, heading toward the castle gate, and only barely slows when Character stumbles and falls, dragged along the rough road. Bloody, bruised and panting, Character gets back to his feet and tries to jog along behind the horse.

Character: Look, it doesn't have to be like this --

Author: I gave you the chance to come here quietly. You really shouldn't argue with your author. It just gives me time to come up with something more interesting to do.

Character: Maybe the woodle pooves wouldn't be so bad --

Author: The group slips through the gate and into the shadows of a courtyard where it seems the sun never reaches. People scurry for the shadows and hide at their approach. Somewhere a man bellows in rage. Loter doesn't pause, as though the place unsettles him. The three head straight into a building filled with cold, damp walls, mold in corners and the sounds of rats running. Salis pushes open a door and they head down the first set of stairs, then another . . . down and down and farther until it seems . . .

Character: *The castle has swallowed him alive.* Yeah, I get it.

Author: Finally, they reach a hall lit by a flickering torch, obviously magically fueled because the cobwebs are so thick no one could have been down this way in a long time. Salis grimaces and uses his sword to cut through them. Decay and death scent the air, and the only sound is hysterical crying from behind a door they pass. "Can I go home now? Please, can I go home?" Loter stops at another door and nods. Salis pries up the rusted metal bar.

Character: I hope he gets tetanus.

Author: The door comes open with a loud wail of unused hinges and Loter shoves Character inside and down to his knees again.

Loter: What's your name, boy? We need it for the records.

Character *looks plaintively at author.*

Author *grabs name books.*

Guards, *anxious to get out of this hellhole, look at author.*

Author: Yes, fine. Right. Okay! I found the name: Varyn!

Character: *(Looks back at the guard)* My name is Varyn.

Loter: We'll write it in the book, Barren --

Character: No, no. Varyn, with a V and a --

Author: The guards slam the door closed. Varyn can hear the bar dropping into place, the guards hurrying away, and the hysterical whisper of someone else: "Can I go home now? Can I go home now?" Varyn leans back, ignoring blood, scrapes and bruises. He knows -- having seen the cobwebs -- that no one is going to come back for a long, long time.

Varyn: *(Bangs head on door a couple times)* This is great. Wonderful. Do you have any clue how you're going to get me back out of here?

Author: Well . . . Do you still have that journey bread?

(End Chapter 5 Notes)

The End

###

About the Author:

Hello!

I am an eclectic and prolific author who publishes in many genres, including Contemporary Fantasy, Epic Fantasy, Science Fiction, Mystery and Young Adult adventures. While I started on the outer edges of traditional publication with sales to small press and magazine publishers, I have since moved most of my work to the Indie world, and I am madly in love with the new era of publishing and the direct contact with readers. Feel free to write me!

I live in Nebraska with my husband, my cats, and a small but entirely useless dog.

Connect with Zette:

Web Site: http://lazette.net

Facebook:
http://www.facebook.com/lazette.gifford

Joyously Prolific Blog: http://zette.blogspot.com/